Merriweather Rides West

Failed law student and ex-outlaw Jacob Merriweather is riding west to start a new life when he strikes up a friendship with Sam Critchley, an eccentric travelling preacher. Sam suggests that they call in at a smallholding owned by his friends Stan and Beth Salinger, only to find that the young couple has been shot dead.

They report the murder to the local sheriff and return to town, where they meet Marie Silversmith, a close friend of the Salingers. Marie is determined to bring the killers to justice and she persuades Jacob and Sam to help her. They are joined by an Indian tracker called Running Deer, and together this unlikely posse sets out on a mission that proves to be both challenging and extremely dangerous!

Merriweather Rides West

Lee Lejeune

A Black Horse Western

ROBERT HALE

© Lee Lejeune 2018
First published in Great Britain 2018

ISBN 978-0-7198-2737-2

The Crowood Press
The Stable Block
Crowood Lane
Ramsbury
Marlborough
Wiltshire SN8 2HR

www.bhwesterns.com

Robert Hale is an imprint
of The Crowood Press

The right of Lee Lejeune to be identified as
author of this work has been asserted by him
in accordance with the Copyright, Designs and
Patents Act 1988

Typeset by
Derek Doyle & Associates, Shaw Heath
Printed and bound in Great Britain by
4edge Limited

CHAPTER ONE

After the incident in Silver Spur, Jacob Merriweather rode north-west towards the North Platte river. He had heard the shots down on the trail, and he knew that someone must have been badly wounded or killed. He didn't know whether it was Marshal Adam Kirk or Steve, and he didn't wait to find out. He just kept riding north-west, heading in the general direction of Oregon. He didn't know much about Oregon, either, but he'd heard it was a land of *milk and honey*. But Merriweather didn't believe in lands of milk and honey, and he didn't rate pots of gold at the end of rainbows, either. Life was life and the earth was the earth, and you had to live with it for better or worse. Jacob Merriweather was a realist.

The episode in Silver Spur had chastened him some-what. He knew that Marshal Adam Kirk might be close on his heels, and he didn't like the notion of swinging from a high tree. So he just kept on riding, stopping occasionally to pull into a stand of trees to check he wasn't being fol-lowed.

Jacob was a restless spirit who didn't care to be reined in. That's why he had left the law practice in the east and ridden west, and that's why he had fallen in with Alphonso and his gang of outlaws. At first, a life robbing banks had appealed to him. It was exciting and stirred up his blood. Alphonso had become a good friend and a loyal buddy, but without his specs he was blind as a bat. He even laughed about it himself! And now Alphonso was lying dead at the funeral directors in Silver Spur with his twisted specs perched on the end of his nose – though Jacob Merriweather didn't know that until somewhat later.

The trouble had started with Black Bart, the huge black-bearded guy who seemed to actually enjoy killing people. As soon as he met Bart, Jacob knew it had been a mistake. Alphonso knew it too, but he went along with it since he had met Bart in the old days when Bart had been a little more civilized. And that unfortunate meeting had sealed Alphonso's death warrant.

'As soon as you meet a killer, you can smell it,' Jacob said to himself. 'That stink comes off him like the stink of rotting corpses! Alphonso should have caught the odour too, but maybe his nasal passages were blocked!'

And so Jacob Merriweather rode on in the direction of Wyoming, with Denver, Colorado, many miles to his left. He knew it would take him weeks to reach Oregon, and that meant camping in the wilderness, which he didn't care for too much, either. His wilderness skills were minimal: he could fry an egg in a pan or a slice of steak, if one was available, but he had never learned to build a shelter, and he had no tent. So he would just have to curl himself up in his bedroll and hope it wouldn't rain or snow! But the fall would soon be here, and that was something of a problem, too.

When a man is alone in the wilderness he learns either to talk to himself or to his horse, or go plumb loco. Jacob had neither horse sense nor horse language, so he just argued with himself and hoped to keep sane.

'You can't go on like this, my friend,' he mumbled. 'Sooner or later something's got to give. So what do you do, my friend?' Jacob called everyone his friend, even if the man was his enemy, so it seemed natural to talk to himself in the same way. 'Maybe you should stop by a cabin some place and ask if there's work available. But there again, what can you do? You've never dug or sowed but you have reaped a bit on other men's land. So, let's get real: you've just been a layabout and a lawbreaker, and the only skills you've mastered are smooth talking and pushing a pen around, and what good are they out here in the wild country?

'Speaking of smooth talking,' Jacob continued to himself, 'It isn't a lot of use talking; you've got to *look* right, too! A hobo or a bum won't cut the mustard even if he does speak like a gent. In fact, as soon as he opens his mouth and starts gobbing forth, folks will think he's just a fraud ready to charm you into submission and rob you of your well-earned green backs. So, what do you advise, my friend?

'Well, one thing's for sure,' he answered himself. 'You need a bath, my friend. Keeping yourself sweet and clean is ace high in my book of good options. And a new outfit of nice-looking dudes might help, too.

'Easy to say, not so easy to do,' Jacob said to his invisible friend. 'Where does a dandy like me find a new suit of clothes around here in the middle of the wilderness and without the dollars to pay for it?

'Ah, there's the rub,' the invisible friend seemed to stroke his beard. 'Why don't you start with a bath. There might not be a hot tub around here but you can always jump into the creek and dunk yourself down. That might be a good starting point. Get rid of all the bugs too!' That was good advice and Jacob followed it through. Every time he came to a creek, he tethered his horse and dunked himself down. His horse looked at him sideways and seemed to grin. 'Horses have a lot more horse sense than we think,' Jacob said to himself.

Then there was the tricky question of food. Jacob had no hunting skills. Since he had come West and met up with Alphonso, he hadn't needed any. The bunch had always stolen their food or caught it in the wild.

His invisible friend said, 'You're a real knucklehead, Jake. Why don't you call in at the local spread and buy some tuck? Surely you've got enough dollars for that!'

Sure! Jacob had a few dollars, but where was the spread? He looked across the endless prairie and saw nothing but sage and creosote and the occasional stand of aspens.

These conversations went on for several days. Jacob had a few supplies so he wasn't exactly starving, but now his belly seemed to be flapping against his ribs more and more urgently.

Then one morning as he was starting to talk to his invisible friend again, he saw a wagon coming towards him on the trail. It was quite a small wagon and it was being drawn by two burros. The wagon was painted in vivid colours as though deliberately inviting attention, and in the driving seat was the squat figure of a gnome-like man with a long white beard – and Jacob guessed it wasn't Santa Claus. It was too early in the year, anyway!

Jacob waited at the side of the trail until the wagon came close and the gnome-like figure drew it to a standstill. The man looked at Jacob and nodded.

'Is this a hold-up?' he asked as casually as a man asking if he was on the road to Paradise. His voice was friendly but somewhat harsh, as though he'd been looking at the world for a long time and decided it was some kind of farce.

'No, my friend,' Jacob assured him. 'This is no hold-up. This is me asking you if you have supplies to spare.'

The parting in the white beard where the lips should be seemed to grin. 'And who is "Me"?' asked the gnome-like figure.

' "Me" is Jacob,' Jacob replied, 'but you can call me Jake if you care to.'

The gnome-like man leaned forwards. 'Pleased to make your acquaintance, Jake. My name's Sam, Sam Critchley.' The driving-seat was too far up, so instead of leaning over to shake Jacob's hand, he just nodded. 'Haven't I seen you someplace before, Jake?'

'I don't think so, Sam,' Jacob replied, 'unless you have second sight.'

Sam nodded again. 'I never forget a face, my friend. That's my ace in the hole and I know I've seen your face before. Those side whiskers of yours are quite distinctive though somewhat bedraggled at the moment. And before you ask again, I do have supplies and I don't carry a gun. So if you have an inclination to shoot me, I guess you can. But I hope you won't because I'm a passing good cook, too. So why don't you join me in some chow? By the way, I see you carry a shooter, and is that a Winchester carbine I see in your saddle holster?'

'Your eyes aren't deceiving you, my friend,' Jacob replied. 'I've carried these tools since I rode West. I heard rumours there are some ugly *hombres* between here and California.'

Sam Critchley gave a rich musical chuckle. 'So you're a gunman?' he suggested.

Jacob grinned back at him. 'I wouldn't claim any such distinction,' he said. 'But a man can't be too careful if he wants to stay alive, can he?'

Sam Critchley gave a hearty laugh again. 'Well, sir, that depends on your business. I've never carried a gun, and so far the Good Lord has kept me in the land of the living.'

'Well, that's really kind of him, I'm sure. But what is your line of business, my friend?'

Sam Critchley nodded like Job on one of his better days. 'Hard to describe,' he said after a moment. 'Mostly it's just talking. And I get along purty well with that. Some folks have called me wise, but I don't take much account of such foolish talk. No man can be called wise until he's dead, as a wise man once said. Or maybe it was happy. I'm not sure about that.'

Jacob chewed that thought over in his mind but made no comment.

Then Sam Critchley spoke again. 'Now listen up, my friend, you look real tuckered out. Why don't I pull in this rig and have a cook up so you can regain your strength and vigour? It's a bit late for breakfast and a little early for lunch but if you don't mind, I don't mind. What do you say?'

Jacob thought, yes please, but he didn't say so.

Sam Critchley climbed down from his painted wagon with surprising agility for such an old man, and he offered his hand to Jacob, and Jacob took it and gave it a good hard squeeze.

'A good firm grip,' Sam Critchley said. 'I like a man with a good strong grip.'

Sam Critchley quickly released his burros from their

harness and they were soon munching away at a patch of grass at the side of the trail. Then he went over to a creek close by and brought back a couple of pails of water for the burros to drink. Jacob's horse raised his head and looked at them askance and then put its head down and went on munching the grass

'I see you wait on those two beasts just like they are human,' Jacob observed.

'Well, of course I do,' Sam Critchley said. 'Those two so-called beasts are like my own children. So I have to be like a father to them. Now to the grub I mentioned.'

Sam Critchley was surpassingly adept and he soon had a fire blazing away beside the trail. He had loaded his cooking pot with various bits of meat and even a few wild onions he'd harvested along the trail, and soon the two men were sitting by the fire chewing away, if not merrily, at least with great satisfaction.

'Where did you get all this from?' Jacob Merriweather asked in surprise.

'From the Indians,' Sam said. 'I have some good Indian amigos, and they taught me a lot about surviving out here in what some ignorant folk call the wilderness. I always carry a little pemmican and jerky around with me so I won't starve.' He even produced a couple of bottles of beer. He removed the tops and handed one to Jacob.

'Now I remember,' he said casually.

'Remember what?' Jacob asked.

'I told you I never forget a face, and I remember where I've seen yours before.'

'Where was that, my friend?' Though Jacob guessed what was coming, he didn't move a muscle.

'You were standing next to Black Bart on a wanted poster. I think it might have been in River Bend.'

Jacob nodded. 'I don't remember where that was taken.'

'But it was you,' Sam insisted. 'Not that it makes no never mind to me. I can read your face like a deck of cards, and I can see pretty well what you're thinking.'

'Then tell me what I'm thinking,' Jacob said.

'You're thinking you've had your fill of shooting and you want to turn your life around.'

Jacob nodded again. 'Well, you're a good reader of faces, my friend.'

Sam was smiling through his beard. 'And I'll tell you something else,' he said. 'I saw a news-sheet the other day, and there was quite a big spread about Black Bart.'

Jacob opened his eyes a little wider. 'So you know what happened to him?'

'I sure do. Black Bart was shot in the leg quite close to his masculinity by a young lady he'd held captive. And a United States Marshal named Adam Kirk arrested him. He's now on trial, and I don't fancy his chances too much. He's a heavy *hombre*, and when he drops through the hangman's trap his head will more than probably snap right off his shoulders. Not that I believe in putting criminals to death, you understand. I'm a man of peace.'

Jacob shrugged his shoulders. He was glad that young Katie Smiley was alive and free, and if anyone had to capture Black Bart, he was pleased it was Marshal Adam Kirk.

After the meal, Sam hitched up his burros and climbed into the driving seat again. 'So why don't you sit up here with me?' he said to Jacob. 'That good horse of yours can trot along beside us. He'll get a little relief from your weight. Not that you're a big man, but lean *hombres* like you are sometimes heavier than they look. And you can

12

doze a little if you fancy it.'

'Where are we headed, my friend?' Jacob asked him.

Sam cocked his head on one side and mused. 'General direction of Fort Laramie, but that's quite a long haul. So I have in mind to call in on some friends of mine, Stan and Beth Salinger. They have a small holding no more than twenty miles from here. Good folks, I think you'll like them. I aim to rest up there for a couple of days or so before riding on. There's a small creek. They have a few cattle and hens, the usual things a small spread can boast of. Stan and Beth have plans to expand, but that's all way ahead in the future, but they're happy to let things grow like the birds and the bees and the crops as the Good Lord sees fit.'

'Sounds like Paradise itself!' Jacob said.

'It's half way to heaven,' Sam agreed.

The rhythm of nature is slow and Sam Critchley went along slowly to keep pace with it. Sure they would stop at Stan and Beth's place, but what was the hurry?

'My opinion is we stop some place I know for tonight and ride in come morning and give our friends a pleasant surprise. What do you say to that, my friend?'

'Sounds like a good idea to me,' Jacob agreed.

So they stopped at a convenient place close to a creek and made camp. Jacob gathered dry sticks and Sam built up a fire, and soon a splendid aroma started pervading the air around the cooking pot.

'It's been a real pleasure meeting like this, Jake,' Sam purred. He had lit up a large curly pipe and was puffing away contentedly by the fire. 'Do you believe in Fate, my friend?'

Jacob grinned at him from across the fire, and the light

of the fire danced on the old man's face, giving it a somewhat devilish appearance.

'Maybe you could tell me what you mean by Fate,' Jacob said. 'Whatever it is, I don't think I've met it before.'

Sam took his pipe out of his mouth and waved it at the stars. 'Do you see those stars up there, Jake?'

'I see them, my friend.'

'What do they say to you, Jake?'

Jacob held his head on one side and looked up at the stars. 'If they're speaking, my friend, I don't hear them.'

Sam was silent for a moment, and then he spoke so quietly that Jacob could scarcely hear what he said. 'You should learn to listen, Jake,' he said.

'And what will I hear?' Jacob asked.

Sam looked at him across the fire. 'Then you'll hear the voice of Fate, my friend.'

Early next morning as the sun was peeping over the horizon to the East, Jacob woke up to find that Sam was already busy cooking eggs and ham.

'You slept in, my friend,' Sam laughed. 'Those burros of mine and that good horse of yours are already itching to be on the trail. My guess is that those two long-eared critters know where we're headed and are looking forward to the welcome. They know more about what's ahead than we could ever know.'

Though Jacob had his doubts about the ability of dumb beasts, he didn't argue; he was too busy bracing himself for his morning dip in the creek.

When he emerged the old man dished out his breakfast, which he attacked with relish.

'We should hit the trail as soon as maybe,' Sam speculated. 'It isn't so far ahead, but the sooner we get there, the

14

better it will be. I'm really looking forward to meeting with Stan and Beth again. They're really the salt of the earth, those two young folk. They're dead set on making a life for themselves out here and they deserve it too. None more so.'

Sam got everything together and soon they were on their way. Twenty miles wasn't far, but Sam didn't believe in hurrying. So they ambled along at a slow but steady pace through a landscape of gently rolling hills and low vegetation. Sam talked as the wagon rolled along, but he didn't say much. Jacob sat beside him on the wagon and surveyed the land. He still felt wary and suspicious that Adam Kirk might be on his tail.

'Lookee there!' Sam pointed towards a low rise.

Jacob looked, but saw nothing in particular. 'What am I looking at?' he asked.

'You see that ridge?' Sam said.

'I see it,' Jacob said.

Sam was smiling under his beard. 'That marks the boundary. When we top the rise you'll see the spread all neat before you, my friend.'

They pushed on to the top of the ridge and saw the cabin. Only it wasn't particularly welcoming. In fact it looked bleak and deserted. Sam drew his team to a halt and reached for his spyglass. 'Well, I'll be damned!' he exclaimed. 'You hear what I hear?'

'I can't hear a thing,' Jacob replied.

'That's what I'm telling you,' Sam said. 'The sound of silence. The place is deserted. No smoke from the fire. No cattle bellowing, no horses neighing, no stock grazing. Just a few hens pecking around.' Sam wrinkled his brow and looked at Jacob with deep concern. 'You know what this means?'

15

'I guess it means your friends Stan and Beth have gone,' Jacob thought, but he didn't say it out of respect for Sam's feelings.

'What it means is that Stan and Beth have vamoosed,' Sam said anxiously, 'and they've taken the stock with them. Now, why would that be?'

'Why don't we take a looksee?' Jacob suggested. He got down from the wagon and drew the Winchester carbine from its sheath.

Sam looked at the Winchester with concern. 'I don't think you need that, my friend.'

Jacob nodded. 'I hope you're right, but I'm taking it anyway.' He hefted the Winchester on to his shoulder and they walked down the hundred metres to the cabin.

'Still and quiet as the grave,' Sam muttered as they approached the door. There was no need to knock or call out – the door was swinging open, and there was obviously no one at home.

'Wait here,' Jacob said. He gave the door a nudge with his Winchester and went inside.

No sign, no sound . . . no one.

Sam followed him in and stared around in astonishment. 'Well, I'll be danged,' he muttered. He went over to the fire pit and bent down, 'Ashes are cold. Those folk haven't been around for some days.'

Jacob peered round the room. It looked domesticated and well lived-in, though somewhat basic. There was even a spinning wheel. He went through to the second room. There was a rough-hewn table with two tin plates on it, but no sign of food. He went through to the third room and saw a bed and a rail with clothes hanging from it. He turned to see Sam standing in the doorway.

'What do you think?' he asked Sam.

16

Sam shook his head. 'I don't like to say what I think. This whole thing is deeply suspicious, two good people suddenly up stakes and leave their property without their valued possessions.' He fixed his eyes on the younger man. 'What do you think?'

Jacob took another look around the room. 'You're not going to like this, but it seems to me like those good people were scared off the property. They were just scared to death. That's what I think.'

Sam Critchley had suddenly become a different man. He drooped at the shoulders, and even his white beard seemed less vibrant. He pulled out a chair and sat down unsteadily. 'What do we do now?' he asked with an air of hopelessness.

'Why don't you rest up for a few minutes and I'll go outside and take a look around?'

Jacob went to the door and looked and listened. Nothing but the sowing of the wind. He went to the wagon and untethered the burros. Then he untied his horse and let it free in the corral. So far so good. He turned to the west and saw the lake. Something drew him towards it, and as he approached he saw the flies and guessed what he was about to find. He braced himself and walked towards the lake, and the flies rose in a vicious swarm.

He went back to the cabin and saw Sam standing in the doorway staring at him.

'Don't tell me what you found,' Sam said. 'I can see it on your face.'

Jacob nodded. 'Dead,' he said flatly. 'Been dead for several days. You don't want to see that, Sam. A man and a woman, both stone dead lying by the lake.'

CHAPTER TWO

Sam looked down at the two bodies and the tears ran from his eyes to the corners of his mouth and mingled with his beard. Jacob put his arm over the old man's shudders to comfort him.

'Tell me,' Sam wailed, 'who would do a thing like this to good, generous people? It's inhuman. Shot in the back of the head, too!'

Jacob looked down at the two corpses. The woman was still leaning forward and the man had fallen to his side after the fatal shot. This wasn't just a killing; it was an execution!

'What do we do now?' Sam asked him.

Jacob wasn't sure. He didn't need to be. He raised his head and looked across the lake and saw three riders and each of them had Winchester rifles pointing in their direction.

'Stay where you are!' one of the men commanded. 'Don't make a move or we might have to shoot you.'

'Don't shoot!' Sam pleaded. 'We come in peace.'

'But do those *hombres* come in peace?' Jacob muttered without lowering his carbine. 'What do you want with us?' he shouted across the lake.

'I think you know what we want!' the man shouted back. 'Just stay where you are and lower your gun if you know what's good for you.'

'I think you should tell us who you are before I do that,' Jacob said.

The man gave a low growl of laughter. 'I'm the sheriff of this county,' he said, 'and I'm investigating a crime. And who are you, and what are you doing here?'

Then Sam shook his beard and spoke out: 'I'm Sam Critchley,' he said. 'I guess you might have heard of me.'

The sheriff nodded. 'I've heard of you, Mr Critchley, and I've seen you speaking in town. And who is this gun-toting friend of yours?' he pointed his gun at Jacob.

'This is a good friend,' Sam piped up. 'We just dropped by to visit our friends Stan and Beth, and came upon this tragic scene.'

'Well,' the Sheriff said. 'You just stay where you are and we'll ride right round.'

The three men mounted their horses and rode round the lake. Jacob lowered his carbine but kept his trigger finger close to the trigger.

The sheriff looked down from his horse and raised his rifle to his shoulder. His two sidekicks looked down at Jacob like he was something dredged up from a polluted river. Jacob grinned back at them and decided he didn't care too much for their style.

'How come you just showed up here, Mr Critchley?' the Sheriff asked in a slightly more amiable tone.

Sam nodded. 'Jake and I have been riding this way together for the last several days or so and we decided to stop by and talk to my friends Stan and Beth, and when we came up on the place we stopped to say hello and this is what we found.'

19

'And since we're talking coincidences here, how come you turned up out of nowhere?' Jacob added.

The sheriff gave a twisted grin. 'That's because it's my job. Mr Whatever your present name happens to be.'

'The name's Merriweather,' Jacob said. 'Jacob Merriweather.'

The sheriff cocked his head on one side. 'And unless I'm very much mistaken you rode with Black Bart, who happens to be on trial for murder in Silver Spur right now.'

'Well, that's true, too,' Jacob confessed, 'but I'm not with him right now. I happen to be here talking to you.'

The sheriff wrinkled his nose and glanced at his sidekicks as if to say, 'We've got a real wise guy here.' 'Well now, Mr Merriweather, I have something of a difficulty here.'

Jacob nodded. 'I think we all have a difficulty here, Sheriff. We've told you why we're here, but we haven't worked out why you and your two amigos are here. Don't you think it might clear the air a little if you told us what brings you to this particular place by the lake at this precise moment? Were you just passing by, or is there some other reason?'

The sheriff paused for a long suspicious moment and then shrugged his shoulders and nodded. 'OK,' he said, 'you made your point. If you and Mr Critchley have been on the trail together for the last several days, you couldn't have been here when these two good people were shot to death.'

'Well now, Sheriff Olsen,' Sam said, 'since we cleared that aside, maybe it would be possible to work together to solve this dreadful crime.'

Sheriff Olsen looked somewhat thoughtful for a while.

Then he seemed to make up his mind. He turned to one of his sidekicks. 'This here is Chuck Yorktown. We call him Yorkie. Why don't you tell these folk what happened, Mr Yorktown?'

Yorkie eased himself in the saddle and looked somewhat nervous. Then he cleared his throat and began to talk in a twittering hillbilly tone.

'I was riding home no more than a few hundred metres away from here when I heard the shots.'

'You heard the shots!' Sam said.

'Yes, I heard the shots loud and clear,' Yorkie agreed.

'When was that?' Sam asked him.

'That was three days back,' Yorkie said. 'That's when I heard the shots,' He looked sort of hangdog and ashamed.

'And did you see anyone?' Jacob asked him.

'Well,' Yorkie said looking even more hangdog. 'I wasn't armed. I had no weapon, so I kept myself quite still.'

'So what happened next?' Jacob asked him.

'Then I heard them riding away. So I pushed forward towards the cabin and that's when I saw these two dead corpses.'

'You say you heard the killers riding away?' Jacob said. 'Like I said, did you see them?'

Yorkie wrinkled up his face and looked round warily as though the killers might be hiding in the brush somewhere close at hand. 'Well, yes, I did sorta see them. They were riding off the stock and I heard them laughing. What sort of man shoots folks dead and then rides off laughing?'

'Someone who enjoys killing,' Jacob suggested. 'And I assure you there are such people.'

'People like Black Bart,' Sheriff Olsen put in.

21

'So what do we do next?' Sam asked.

'If I might make a suggestion,' the second sidekick said in a thickly accented voice. Jacob glanced at him and realized he was part Indian.

'This here is Running Deer Johnson,' Sheriff Olsen introduced. 'He's the best tracker from here to the Rocky Mountains. What is your suggestion, Running Deer?'

Running Deer looked at Jacob with a half smile as though he thought Jacob was the only one in the group with an ounce of savvy. 'The first thing we do is we give these poor dead souls a decent burial.'

'You mean like we hoist them on to a wagon and drive them into town?' Sheriff Olsen said.

'Since we haven't got a wagon and these poor stiff corpses are beginning to stink something bad, the best thing to do is to bury them here on the property. I guess they won't complain about that. And if you want, we can put up a cross to mark the spot.'

Everyone looked at Sam who, they thought, was the authority on such matters. Sam tugged his beard as if to make his thoughts flow free. Then he wagged his head. 'I guess that's the best thing to do,' he said. 'We can wrap the bodies in whatever we can find and give them a respectful burial. I guess that's what they would prefer.'

They found the necessary tools in the outhouse and got to work on the graves. Running Deer and Yorkie did most of the digging, and old Sam made a passable cross to erect over the site. Then they all stood round with their hats in their hands and their heads bowed as Sam said a few well chosen words, after which Running Deer chanted an Indian song for the dead that none of the others could understand.

It was now well into the afternoon and they gathered

round Sam's rig while he cooked up a meal. Although burying folks who had been dead for three days was a somewhat gruesome task it didn't take the edge off their appetites, and they all chewed away with gusto.

'Now, boys,' Sheriff Olsen said, 'we need to ride back to town before sunset or camp right here and wait till morning.'

Sam shook his head. 'Well, sir, I'd like to look inside the cabin and search for evidence. The killers must have had a reason, and I aim to find out what it is.'

'Maybe I should join you in that,' Olsen said. 'The sooner we get on the trail of those killers the better.'

'That's good thinking, Sheriff,' Running Deer piped up. 'And while you're doing that maybe I should look for signs. Three men on horseback shouldn't be too hard to track even after three days, and we can round up any stray cattle we come across.'

Jacob chose to go with Running Deer, and it didn't take long to find the cattle since they were grazing not far from the spread. There were six head of cattle.

'Well, that was easy enough ,' Jacob said. 'What do we do with these beasts?'

'Leave them here to look after themselves,' Running Deer said. 'But take a look at this.' He dismounted and knelt down on the ground.

Jacob got down from his horse and looked at the signs. 'What do you read, my friend?' he asked.

Running Deer straightened up. 'I see five horses,' he said. 'Three with men on them, the other two being led.'

'So the killers took the horses with them.' Jacob said.

Running Deer looked at him and grinned. 'That was a damned fool thing to do, because stolen horses show up somewhere sooner or later and the *hombres* who did those

23

killings will show up with them.'

Running Deer mounted up again and rode on quite slowly, examining the ground for signs and he soon stopped his horse and dismounted. 'Lookee here,' he said, holding up a small discarded bottle and then a small brown object. He handed the brown stub to Jacob. 'One of the killers smokes small brown cigaritos.' He held the empty bottle to his nose and sniffed. 'Cheap whiskey,' he said, 'like the hooch they sell to the Indians. It makes them mad!' He handed the bottle to Jacob who took a sniff.

'That stuff would drive anyone crazy,' Jacob concluded.

'Good we found these,' Running Deer said, as he stowed away the evidence in a leather bag. 'Those killers were mad or drunk.'

'And they were also careless,' Jacob added. 'So what do we do now, my friend? Do we go on tracking them down?'

Running Deer pulled a sceptical face. 'We could track them all the way to Kingdom Come and back, but then what do we do, shoot it out with them?'

'So we go back and report to the sheriff?' Jacob said.

'I guess that's what we must do,' Running Deer agreed.

That night all five of them sat round a fire Sam had built up not too far from the cabin. Nobody wanted to take shelter in the cabin since they thought it might be somewhat spooky!

Come sun-up Sam was astir. He had been over to the cabin and found a few more supplies, and they all enjoyed a full hearty breakfast, after which Sheriff Olsen called what he described as a 'Council of War'.

'Now, Mr Critchley, how do you figure this?' he asked.

Sam looked at the fire and then up at the sky. Then he

shook his head. 'Well now, Sheriff, I've been thinking on that.'

'And what conclusions have you come up with?'

'Well, I have to confess this whole thing has thrown me way off balance. But one thing's for sure, we must catch those cold-blooded killers before they kill other folk.'

There was a murmur of approval from the others. For some reason known only to himself Jacob was particularly keen to track down these cold-blooded killers. Maybe it was the thought of Black Bart's ruthlessness that made him eager to track them down, or some other reason, he couldn't be sure. But whatever it was, the sight of that cigarito stub and the reek of that hooch whiskey had stiffened his resolve.

They rode back along the trail until they came within sight of the township of Buffalo Bluffs close to the River Platte and no more than ten miles from the murder scene.

'Are you boys coming into town?' Sheriff Olsen asked them.

'I think I'll just set up camp right by the river,' Sam said. 'That's my usual place. I need to think a bit and meditate on what's happened, and for that it's best to be alone.'

'In which case,' Jacob said,' I guess I should ride into town and find some place to bed down and maybe have a bath.'

'Well, there's a good hotel in town. They call it The Grand. And since it's the only decent hotel in town I guess it's the grandest you're gonna get,' the sheriff said.

'In that case, I guess I'll have to put up with it,' Jacob reflected.

'Come to my office in the morning,' Olsen said. 'I think we might have a few things to talk over.'

*

Jacob hitched his horse to the hitching rail outside The Grand hotel where it could take a drink from the trough. The hotel ran to two floors and it had a sign in gold letters proclaiming it 'The Grand'. He stepped inside and looked around. There was a long bar with a man sitting behind it reading a news-sheet. Apart from that the place was still and quiet, almost peaceful. There were two or three tables to left and right, and two were occupied. Several pairs of eyes looked up at him and then looked down again. He walked over to the bar and rested his hands on it. For a long moment there was no response. He could hear a fly buzzing around somewhere, but the news-sheet remained still.

'Good day,' Jacob said. 'Anyone at home?'

After a second the news-sheet stirred and a bespectacled face peered at him. 'Yes?' an unwelcoming voice barked out.

'Just wanted to ask you,' Jacob said.

The news-sheet moved further to one side. 'Ask me what?' the voice demanded abruptly.

'Ask you if you have a room,' Jacob said.

'A room?' The news-sheet disappeared and a man materialized and came forward. 'How many nights?' he asked.

'That depends.'

The man thrust a ledger at him. 'Sign here.' He placed an index finger on the space. 'That'll be two dollars a night including breakfast. Two bits extra if you want water brought up for a bath.' He looked up and glared at Jacob. 'Will you be taking a bath?'

'How about dinner? Do you do dinner?' Jacob asked.

The bartender gave him a keen scrutiny. 'Dinner will be extra.'

'Put me down for dinner,' Jacob said. 'And I'll take a bath as soon as the water's ready.'

'Tub's in the room. I'll bring up the water as soon as it's heated.' He reached up and selected a key. 'Room twelve – up the stairs, second door on the right. And take your horse to the barn back of the hotel. Hank will take care of it. He likes horses better than human folk.' A thin smile appeared fleetingly on his face. 'And with good reason, too.'

Jacob led his horse to the barn and handed it over to Hank, who couldn't have been more than twelve years old. 'Give him the best,' Jacob said.

The boy smiled at him pleasantly. 'Oh, I always give them the best, sir!' he sang out.

Jacob pressed a coin into his hand.

'Why, thank you, good sir!' the boy crowed.

The bartender might not have been the most sociable of critters, but at least he was prompt. Jacob hadn't been in his small box of a room for more than ten minutes before there was a rap on the door and the bartender carried in two buckets of water. 'Take good care,' he said, 'the water's real hot!' He poured the water into the tub, where it steamed. 'I'll bring cold and you can add it according to your taste.'

Jacob had ordered a bath, but the tub was so small that he couldn't possibly stretch out in it; the best he could do was crouch with his knees bent and soak himself. The Grand did, however, provide soap, so he could soap himself down.

When the bartender brought up two buckets of cold water Jacob had already stripped down to his underpants and was wielding a cut-throat razor. He shaved cautiously, taking care not to spoil his mutton-chop whiskers. Then he stepped into the tub and dunked himself down as best as he could.

He stayed in that semi-foetal position so long that he almost fell asleep. Then he shook his head and climbed out of the tub and dried himself down.

When he had dressed he stretched out on his bed and almost immediately fell into a deep sleep. He dreamed of the two good people lying dead by the lake. But in the dream they weren't dead. The man turned over to face him and laughed. Jacob woke with a start, and realized that what he thought had been the laugh of a dead man was the laugh of someone on the floor below. He rolled out of bed and looked at himself in the mirror, which was yellow and cracked. It reflected a man who was spruce and clean. So Jacob combed his hair and his whiskers, and went downstairs to the dining room. To his surprise he found old Sam Critchley waiting for him.

Sam smiled. 'So, I thought I'd ride into town and give myself a treat. D'you mind if I join you?'

'Glad to welcome you,' Jacob said. 'What's on your mind?'

'There's a whole heap of things spinning round in there just like shirts in a tub,' Sam said. 'Thought you might like to help me rinse them through.'

They sat down at their table, and the waiter-cum-bartender came over to take their order, and this time he was a lot more cordial. 'Good evening, Mr Critchley,' he said. 'I guess you'd like the steak, and we've got potatoes and a little cabbage to go with it. Would that suit you?' His eyes switched to Jacob. 'You're looking real spruced up, Mr Merriweather. Hope you enjoyed the tub.'

'You want the truth, it was a little cramped for my long

legs,' Jacob said.

The bartender gave a thin smile and leaned towards Sam confidentially. 'I just heard the terrible news, Mr Critchley.'

Sam nodded. 'Such good young folk, too.'

'You think they'll catch the killers?' the bartender asked.

'Oh, they'll catch them right enough,' Sam said. 'All shall be revealed, my good man.'

Jacob looked at the bartender. 'When I was drinking earlier I noticed you had a glass of brown cigaritos on the bar.'

'Yes, sir, we do. Would you like me to get one for you? I'm sure they go well with a good juicy steak.'

Jacob smiled politely, 'I just wanted to ask you, do you have much passing trade in those cigaritos?'

'Well, yes, sir, as a matter of fact we do.'

Jacob tapped on the table. 'Will you take your mind back a week or two and tell me, have you sold any of those cigaritos recently?'

The bartender smirked. 'People buy them all the time, sir.' He looked past Jacob in the direction of the door. 'But now you come to mention it, a bunch of guys dropped by a week or two ago. They drank a deal of whiskey and one of them took a whole lot of those cigaritos. I guess it might have been a dozen or so.'

'How many?' Jacob asked him.

'Like I said, a dozen or so.'

'I mean how many men?'

'Oh!' the barman said. 'I guess that would be three.'

Jacob looked at Sam who shook his head. 'You seen these men before?' Sam asked.

The bartender looked thoughtful. 'Can't recall I have.'

'Could you describe these men?' Jacob asked him.

The bartender looked towards the door again as though trying to form a picture in his mind. 'As I recall it, they were wearing range clothes. Could have been waddies, and they were packing guns.' He gave a wry grin. 'Oh yes, and one of them bought a bottle of whiskey to take away.'

Jacob looked at Sam, and Sam nodded again.

'Shall I order your grub, good sirs?' the bartender asked

'That'll be fine, my friend,' Jacob replied.

'Like I surmised,' Sam said to Jacob, 'the truth always comes out sooner or later, and in this case it might be a lot sooner than we expected.'

After the meal they walked over to the sheriff's office. Olsen was still at his desk and Running Deer was with him. Olsen looked up with a frown. 'It's all over town,' he said solemnly.

'I'm sure it is,' Sam said. 'You've had a good many shoot-outs in town, but this is quite different.'

'We're looking for three killers, one of them with a particular liking for brown cigaritos,' Olsen said.

Jacob told Olsen and Running Deer about his conversation with the bartender. 'It looks like these three strangers showed up in town just about the time of the killings,' he said. 'It might have been the same day.'

There was a moment of silence. Olsen looked slightly pained as though he thought the whole thing was sliding out of his control. 'We have to find those three killers,' he said quietly.

'Well,' Running Deer said, 'Those *hombres* fired the shots, but they weren't the killers.'

The other three looked at Running Deer. 'What d'you

mean by that?' the sheriff asked him.

Running Deer gave a tight smile. 'Those three *hombres* were hired by someone else, and that someone must have a real dark hatred for the two victims.'

Sam nodded sagely. 'Running Deer's right,' he said. 'And that *hombre* might not be too far off. He or she might be sitting right here in town.'

CHAPTER THREE

Jacob Merriweather sat in the bar of the Grand hotel and thought things over.

'What have I got myself into here?' he said to himself. 'I'm riding towards the golden land of Oregon where the sun shines every day and they grow some of the finest apples on earth. What the hell am I doing here, in the middle of nowhere, trying to work out who killed two innocent people no more than a week back?'

He took a sip of the really bad whiskey he'd ordered and looked across at Sam Critchley, who was sipping a fruit drink of some kind. 'Listen, my friend,' he said. 'What do you aim to do about this business?'

Sam tugged at his beard. 'Well, now, Jake, I don't think I have much choice. I need to find out who killed my two friends and bring them to justice.'

'Even if they hang high on the gallows?'

'Well,' the old man said 'I don't believe in death by hanging, but justice is justice. By the way, Jake, I heard they hung Black Bart. Did you know that? Someone said a man in the crowd shouted out abuse and Bart opened his mouth to reply, but it was too late: at that moment, the hangman opened the trap and Black Bart dropped down.

They say that he weighed a ton, so his neck must have snapped immediately. Can you believe that? Dying with a blaspheming word on your lips?'

Jacob felt a chill wind sweeping through the bar and ruffling the hairs at the back of his neck.

'How do you aim to bring those killers to justice, my friend?' he asked the old man.

Sam held up his hand. 'Patience,' he said. 'The mills of God grind slow, but they grind exceeding fine. Haven't you a-heard that?'

'That may well be so,' Jacob said, 'but while those mills are grinding, what are we going to do about keeping our bodies and souls together? I can't afford to live here in grand style for more than a few days. I just don't have the wherewithal.'

The old man grinned at him across the table. 'All you soft folk think about is bodily comforts. If you get low in cash just come down to the river and pitch camp close to my wagon. The grass is lush there, so the burros seem contented. And I have supplies enough for a week or two.' Sam paused to stroke his white beard and then added, 'I shall be holding a meeting tomorrow just before sunset at the end of Main Street. Why don't you join me and pass round the hat? You'd be surprised how many folks are prepared to dig into their britches for the good of their souls.'

Jacob was still smiling. 'So you are some kind of travelling preacher?' he said.

Sam held his head on one side. 'I guess you could put it like that. Some folks think I have the healing touch, but I don't boast about that. It sets people's hopes too high.' He gave a low chuckle.

Jacob nodded and thought, Is this old man a genuine preacher or is he a fraud with a golden tongue like some sort of quack doctor? He put down his poisonous hooch and stood up. 'I think I'll just walk to the end of town and back, take a look at the place.'

'Good idea,' Sam said. 'It's always advisable to check out a town. You can learn a lot about a place that way. It's like there's something in the air, you know.'

Jacob raised his hand and stepped out on to the side-walk. He looked both ways and then across the street where Sheriff Olsen stood in the shade watching him. That sonofabitch with the star doesn't trust me an inch, he thought.

He stepped off the sidewalk and walked over to Olsen. 'Good day to you, Sheriff,' he greeted.

Olsen flicked away the butt of the quirly he'd been smoking and gave Jacob a half smile. 'So what are your immediate plans, Mr Merriweather?'

'My immediate plans are to stay alive,' Jacob said. 'I just go along from day to day and try to take account of what drifts my way.'

'That might be a good policy as far as it goes, Mr Merriweather, but how far does it go?'

Jacob turned his head towards the end of town. 'It might go as far as Oregon,' he said, 'but right now the end of Main Street could be far enough.'

He walked slowly to the end of town and looked out into the distance. Somewhere out there is a trail that runs all the way to Oregon. All I need to do is go back and get my horse and ride out of town. What is there to keep me here? He looked out across the purple sage and stood in contemplation for a moment. Then he turned right round and started walking back into town.

It was a sleepy place in the middle of nowhere and there weren't many folk on the street. He heard voices to his right, and looking towards the sidewalk, he saw a bunch of womenfolk talking together. He paused and looked in their direction. Then they dispersed, leaving only one of them standing on the sidewalk to stare at him. She was wearing a bonnet against the glare of the sun. As he walked towards her she gave a curtsey.

'Good day to you, ma'am,' he said raising his hat. 'Seems like a fine day.'

'Good day to you, sir,' she said, meeting his eye.

He saw that she was quite young, maybe in her early twenties, and she had auburn curls peeping down from her bonnet and her eyes were blue and challenging.

'So you live here in town?' he asked her.

The young woman nodded. 'I saw you yesterday with Sam Critchley, the preacher man.'

'I guess that might be so,' he replied with a smile.

Her face clouded over. 'I'm told you found Beth and Stan Salinger dead by the lake.'

Jacob nodded. 'We buried them on the spread. How well did you know Beth and Stan?'

'Everyone here in town knew them. They were good people, and Beth was my special friend. I used to go out to the farm and spend the day with her when I could.'

'It must be hard for you, Miss. . . .'

'Marie Silversmith,' she said.

'Well, now, Miss Silversmith, I guess you'd like to see those killers caught.'

She smiled sadly. 'They must be brought to justice, Mr Merriweather,' she said.

Jacob gave a slight start. 'So, how come you know my name, Miss Silversmith?'

She nodded. 'I heard it around town. You stay here for an hour, everyone knows everything about you. I heard tell

35

you're a gunman and I see you carry a gun.' She looked at him steadily, challengingly, for a moment.

Jacob smiled again. 'Well, Miss Silversmith, you don't want to believe everything you hear, do you?'

She was still staring at him boldly. 'I believe what I see, Mr Merriweather,' she said.

'And what do you see, Miss Silversmith?'

'I see a tall man with a friendly smile and a gun on his hip.'

Jacob gave a slight bow. 'Well, that's a fair summary, I guess. It's been a pleasure talking to you. I think I'll make my way back to the hotel.' He put his hat on and started in the direction of the Grand hotel.

'Just one thing,' he heard her say as he started to walk on.

He turned and looked at her. 'Yes, Miss Silversmith?'

She creased her brow. 'Those men who killed my friends. I think I saw them.'

He stepped towards her again. 'You think you saw them?'

'A few days back. It must have been about the time Beth and Stan were murdered.'

Jacob nodded. 'I guess a lot of people must have seen them, Miss Silversmith. Can you remember what they looked like?'

She pursued her lips in thought. 'At the time it occurred to me that they were just three ranch hands passing through.'

'Old or young?'

'As I recall, two were young and the other one was middle-aged. And they carried guns, like you.'

'Nothing unusual about that,' Jacob smiled. 'Quite a lot of men out here on the frontier carry guns, especially cattle ranchers.'

For some reason that made Miss Silversmith smile, and he noted that she had a charming smile that went well with her melodious voice. She fixed her blue challenging eyes on him. 'Mr Merriweather, I wonder if you'll be kind enough to do something for me?'

He raised his Stetson again. 'Of course, Miss Silversmith. It will be a pleasure.'

She hesitated for a second. 'I'd like to visit their graves. I want to honour my friends.' Then she looked at him directly. 'I'm not sure I can go on my own. So I wonder if you'd be kind enough to escort me?'

He stood with his hat in his hand staring at her for a moment. 'You mean you want a gunman to escort you to visit the graves of your friends?' he asked.

She looked down and her cheeks became a somewhat enhanced pink. 'Not as a gunman, Mr Merriweather, but as an honourable gentleman.'

Jacob couldn't remember being called honourable before. So he gave a slight bow. 'It will be a pleasure to escort you, Miss Silversmith. Shall we say tomorrow morning at around eight, or is that too early?'

She looked up at him again. 'That will suit me just fine, Mr Merriweather.'

Jacob walked back towards the Grand hotel and thought of his own words to Sheriff Olsen half an hour earlier: 'I just go along from day to day and try to take account of what drifts my way.'

In fact what had drifted his way was a whole lot more substantial than drifting tumbleweed. It had come in the form of a highly attractive young woman with very challenging eyes.

He went into the hotel and checked out. 'You leaving so

soon, Mr Merriweather?' the bartender asked him.

'Urgent business,' Jacob replied.

He gathered his things together and walked round to the stable to pick up his horse. Hank the stable boy gave him a cheery smile. 'That's a real fine horse, sir,' he said. 'I gave him my best, and he appreciated it!'

Jacob pressed another coin into the boy's hand and the boy bowed low. 'Why, thank you, sir. That is most generous of you.'

Jacob patted him on the shoulder. 'You been to school?' he asked.

A melancholy look clouded the boy's face. 'Oh, no sir, nothing like that. I wanted to, but my folks couldn't raise the fees.'

Jacob mounted his horse and rode towards the river where he found old Sam Critchley beside a fire cooking up something in his black pot. His two burros were grazing contentedly close by. He looked up and gave Jacob a welcoming smile. 'I knew you'd come,' he said.

Jacob grinned. 'Couldn't stand that hogwash they call whiskey. If I ever get rich enough I'll open my own saloon and sell good honest whiskey.'

He dismounted and let his horse join Sam's two burros. Then he squatted by the fire and told Sam he had met a certain young lady named Marie Silversmith.

Sam nodded. 'I know the lady in question. Been to one or two of my meetings. Seems to enjoy talking about important matters such as who we are, where do we come from, and where are we going.'

Jacob told the old man how she had asked him to escort her to the murdered couple's graves and that he'd agreed.

Sam held his head on one side and chuckled. 'Well,

take care, young man. The one thing they know in this town is how to talk, and ignorant folk are quick to draw conclusions. Though I guess they also know Miss Silversmith is an independent spirit. Some even say she has special powers like a witch.'

'What do you think about that?' Jacob asked him.

Sam smiled. 'I haven't seen any sign of witchcraft myself – but then again, maybe I'm too old to notice.'

Next morning early, Sam cooked up a real fine breakfast and he and Jacob sat by the fire and enjoyed it.

'Well, my friend,' Sam said, 'don't ask for my advice because I won't give it. Just take care of yourself and that strong-headed young woman, and see you get back safely.' He looked up at the sky. 'And take account of what the Good Book says: "Red sky in the morning, shepherd's warning" – that sky over there to the east looks a little red to me. So take care, my friend.'

They shook hands and Jacob mounted up and rode towards town.

When he hit town it was bang on eight o'clock in the morning and the first thing he saw was a figure riding towards him, and it was Marie Silversmith – but what a different Marie Silversmith she was! She was dressed in range clothes just like a man, and she was wearing a wide Stetson hat.

As she approached she raised her hand and said, 'Good day, Mr Merriweather, you're right on time.'

He drew in beside her and they rode together.

'I've brought food,' she said, 'in case we get hungry.'

'That's mighty kind of you, Miss Silversmith,' he said. He noticed she sat well in the saddle, as though she was used to riding. No side-saddle stuff. Just a young woman riding like a man. From a distance she might have been mistaken for a slim, good-looking young *hombre*.

'I've been meaning to ask you something,' he said. 'What about your folks? Do they know what you're doing, riding out of town with a notorious gunman?'

She smiled under her Stetson. 'No, they don't, Mr Merriweather.' She looked at him out of the corner of her eye. 'They don't know because they've passed on.'

'Passed on,' he repeated.

She nodded. 'They passed on some years back.'

'Really! So you're alone in the world.'

She didn't volunteer any further information. So he rode on without speaking for a while.

'How is it for you in town ?' he asked after a while.

She nodded and smiled. 'I'm thinking of leaving, Mr Merriweather, and that's the truth. A woman in this town is either married or a whore. And I'm neither, so they treat me with suspicion and think I'm a witch, and that protects me . . . at least for the moment.' She turned to him again. 'They probably think I've cast a spell on you, Mr Merriweather.'

Jacob grinned. 'Well, maybe they're wiser than you think, Miss Silversmith.'

It was a short ride to the spread, and as soon as they got there, she stopped and looked at the place. 'Looks strange, Mr Merriweather, doesn't it? You can always tell when there's nobody at home, can't you?'

She dismounted and led her horse over to the grave and looked down. Jacob remained mounted, though he removed his Stetson in respect.

Marie stood at the graveside and bared her head and looked down. Then she knelt and began to recite 'The Lord is my Shepherd. . . .' in a clear but sad tone. Her horse whinnied, and then stood in silence as if it understood. Jacob found the scene strangely moving.

Marie stood for a long time looking down at the mound where the two were buried. Then she rose and drew back. 'This should never have happened,' she said quietly.

Jacob dismounted and moved forward and stood slightly behind her, and waited for what seemed a very long time. Then she turned and he saw tears in her eyes. 'Thank you,' she said. 'That was a kind thing to do.'

Jacob felt impelled towards her but he stood still and said nothing.

'I have to tell you something, Mr Merriweather,' she said.

Jacob nodded.

'I knew as soon as I knelt down by the grave.'

'What did you know?' he asked quietly.

She breathed in slowly. 'I know who committed this heinous crime. You might think like the others that I'm a witch, but as I knelt there came a voice loud and clear, and it spoke the name of the killer.'

Jacob kept silent or a moment. 'You want to tell me the name, Miss Silversmith?' he murmured.

'I think we should eat,' she said after a pause. 'I think we should go up to the cabin.'

'Are you happy with that?' he asked.

'If you mean do I believe in ghosts?' she said, 'I keep an open mind on that subject. But I know one thing: my friends Beth and Stan wouldn't haunt anyone. But Beth did speak to me just now by the grave. Do you believe that?'

Jacob wasn't sure what he believed. Maybe he never had. But he said, 'I believe anything you say, Miss Silversmith.'

They led their horses to the barn, which had a good

supply of hay. Then they went to the door of the cabin. Jacob pushed it open and went inside. All was deathly quiet, except for a slight rustling, which might have been a rat. 'Come right in, Miss Silversmith,' he said.

Marie walked in and sniffed the air. 'Someone's been here,' she said.

Jacob was surprised, not by what she said, but by the keenness of her senses. No wonder some folks thought she was a witch!

'You're probably right,' he said, 'but whoever they were, they're not here now.'

'Sit down, Mr Merriweather. It's time to eat.'

They sat down at the pine table and Marie produced a pack of food.

'Pardon me, Miss Silversmith. Before we go any further, since you asked me to escort you, would you mind calling me Jacob or Jake? Mr Merriweather sounds a little stiff and formal, don't you think?' He looked at her across the table and saw her face turn a deeper shade of pink.

'I quite like Jacob,' she said. 'It sounds kind of biblical.'

Jacob was smiling to himself. 'Well, I'm no saint. But maybe I could call you Marie?' he suggested.

'I'd like that, Jacob.'

After the meal Jacob glanced at her across the table. 'Since you've allowed me to escort you, Marie, maybe you'd be kind enough to tell me what your dead friend told you by the graveside?'

Marie looked down at the table and said nothing for a moment. 'It was a name, Jacob. I heard a name.'

'So,' he said, 'would you care to tell me the name?'

She opened her mouth to speak but then froze. They both heard the sound of a horse whinnying from close by.

Jacob rose quickly to his feet. 'Stay right there!' he said.

He drew his gun and went to the door.

He saw a man sitting on a horse looking down at the grave. Was it in contemplation or curiosity? Jacob wondered. The man turned to look at him in surprise, and then drew his gun and fired. The bullet splintered the door jamb inches above Jacob's head, and Jacob ducked. Then he levelled his gun and fired. As he fired, the man spurred his horse forward and Jacob missed.

The man turned in the saddle and fired again, but missed by a yard.

Jacob cocked his gun and held it above his shoulder. Now the rider was galloping away hell for leather – Jacob could have taken another shot, but at that distance the chance of hitting his target was minimal.

'Now I know,' Marie said from beside him.

'What do you know?' he asked between clenched teeth.

Marie was breathing hard. 'That was one of the men I saw in town just before my friends were murdered.'

'I guessed that might be so,' Jacob said.

'And that's not all,' she said. 'That man was riding Stan's horse.'

He turned to her quickly. 'Are you sure?'

She nodded. 'I'd know that horse anywhere. It had a white blaze just above its muzzle, narrow at the base and widening towards the ears. And it was a chestnut colour. Stan loved that horse.'

'So,' Jacob said, 'they say a dog always returns to its vomit and a murderer always returns to the scene of his crime, which means that guy was the killer.'

'Except that he wasn't,' Marie said.

Jacob checked his revolver and returned it to its holster. 'He won't come back,' he told her. 'If he hadn't been moving, I'd have winged him. Now why don't we sit down and you can tell me what your dead friend said to you?'

Marie sat down and looked decidedly agitated. 'She spoke the name Jack Davidson,' she said.

'Jack Davidson,' Jacob repeated. 'Is that supposed to mean something?'

'That's the name of the man who hired those killers. One of them, probably the one we've just seen, fired the shots, but the man who hired them was Jack Davidson.'

Jacob nodded three times. 'And who is this man Davidson?'

Marie looked at him squarely. 'Jack Davidson runs the Circle Bar Ranch, some twenty miles west of here. He's the biggest rancher in the territory.'

'But why should he want those two good people dead?' Jacob asked.

Her challenging eyes met his. 'Revenge,' she said.

'Revenge?' he murmured.

'Yes, revenge,' she repeated.

Jacob went to the door and looked around. 'Why don't we sit out here on the bench while you tell me about Jack Davidson and revenge? If that killer comes back, which I doubt, we don't want to be trapped like rats in here, do we?'

They sat side by side on the bench, and Jacob looked up at the sky and remembered what old Sam had said: 'Red sky in the morning, shepherd's warning!' Although the sun was shining brightly, the sky to the east looked kind of angry.

'There's going to be rain,' Marie said. 'I can smell it in the air.'

'I can smell it too,' he said. 'Too late to start back to town now. So, why don't you just tell me about revenge?'

*

Marie was an intelligent young woman and she told the story with great fluency. Apparently, several years earlier when Beth was only sixteen, she had been offered in marriage to the big rancher Jack Davidson. Her pa and ma thought it would give her a good start in the world. But she couldn't stand Jack Davidson, who was almost old enough to be her grandfather, and was a bully. But then she had fallen in love with Stan Salinger who was working as a wrangler on the ranch.

'So they ran away together and settled down here. I guess they thought Jack Davidson would never find them. But they underrated Davidson, and they couldn't have guessed he was revengeful enough to want them dead.' She looked steadily at Jacob. 'So that's the story. The question is, what do we do about it?'

'That's a big question,' Jacob replied. 'And right now I don't think I can come up with the answer.' He looked up at the darkening sky and saw a flash of lightning. 'A summer storm,' he said. 'I think we'll have to sit right here until it clears.'

CHAPTER FOUR

It was more than a summer storm; it went on for more than an hour and the rain came down like stair rods. Jacob and Marie went into the cabin and sat at the pine table.

'Well, Miss Marie, it looks like we might have to stay here all night.'

'Indeed, we might,' she agreed with a smile.

'And what will the good folk of town think about that?' he speculated.

'Those good folk can think what they like,' she said. 'And they probably do anyway.'

But then the rain eased off and the birds began to twitter outside. They went out to the barn and saddled up the horses. Marie stood by the grave and said another prayer, and they set off back to town.

'So what do we now, Mr Jacob?' she asked him.

'I've been thinking about that, Miss Marie, and I've been wondering why that *hombre* returned to the scene of the crime.'

'And what are your conclusions on that, Mr Jacob?'

'Well, I guess it wasn't the need to repent. And another thing, why did he come alone?'

'And riding on Stan's horse, too,' she said.

'So many questions and not many answers,' Jacob speculated.

Marie nodded. 'They say two heads are better than one. So why don't we put our thoughts together, Mr Jacob?'

'So what do you think, Miss Marie?'

Marie paused for a moment. 'I think this man took his pay and rode off the ranch. He came back to the scene of the crime to look for something and found us there.'

'And he came alone because there's been some kind of bust-up between him and Jack Davidson or the other killers,' Jacob added.

'That man Davidson may be a smart cowman, but he's a jealous fool!' Marie said vehemently.

'A killer and a fool! Why do you say that, Marie?'

'Because if you want your dirty work done, either you do it yourself or you hire one man to do it. If you hire four men, they're going to fall out sooner or later, and probably sooner.'

Jacob looked at her for a moment and she looked back. He thought, This young woman has a fine brain, you know that, Jake?

Now they were on the edge of town, and to Jacob's surprise it was bustling with activity. On the left close to the Grand hotel a tent with red and white stripes had been erected, and under it was a small dais or platform. Men and women were busy putting out chairs for an audience. Like most main streets in the West, the street was wide, so there was plenty of room for riders and buggies to pass by.

'They're getting ready for Sam Critchley's event,' Marie told him. 'Everyone will be looking forward to it.'

'So you've heard him before?'

'Oh, I've heard him many times,' she said with a smile. 'Sam has the gift of tongues. I've seen women cry out and faint as he speaks. And he has the healing touch as well. He just lays his hand on a person's head and they feel a whole lot better.'

'So you really believe that stuff?' Jacob marvelled.

She was smiling at him. 'I not only believe it, I've felt it,' she affirmed.

As they rode on, they saw Sheriff Olsen standing a little beyond the striped tent with a quirly on his lip. 'So you're back in town,' he said with a suggestive grin. 'What took you so long?'

'What took us so long,' Jacob said, 'was there was a storm. Maybe you didn't notice it, Sheriff?'

A gleam of malice appeared in Olsen's eye. 'So you took shelter in the cabin,' he said.

'And someone took a shot at us,' Marie added.

Olsen looked startled. 'Someone took a shot at you?' he said.

Marie nodded. 'I think it might have been one of the men who killed Beth and Stan.'

'Are you sure about that, Miss Silversmith?'

'Sure as I can be, Sheriff. He was riding Stan's horse.'

Olsen took a step towards them. 'Is this the truth you're telling me?'

'Either it's the truth,' Jacob said, 'or we've had a joint vision, but that *hombre* was no phantom. Those bullets came real close. You come up to the cabin and I'll show you where a bullet hit the door frame.'

For the first time Olsen looked really interested. 'You'd better come over to the office and fill me in on the details.'

They sat in the sheriff's office and Marie did most of the talking. She was a good talker, and spoke straight to the point without frills or unnecessary details. Jacob sat back and admired her skills. Olsen listened intently and nodded several times and jotted down a few notes. Then he shook his head and looked at Marie gravely. 'Are you telling me that Jack Davidson hired those killers, Miss Silversmith?'

'Yes, I am, Mr Olsen,' she replied with dignity.

Olsen put down his pen and gave her a straight look. 'You realize what you're saying, Miss Silversmith?'

'I think I do, Sheriff,' she replied without flinching.

Olsen frowned. 'You must know that Jack Davidson is one of the biggest ranchers in the territory. His father John Davidson started the business in the early days when cattle ranching was a really profitable business.'

Then Jacob spoke for the first time. 'Do you know Jack Davidson, Sheriff?'

Olsen turned slowly to face Jacob. 'Not personally, Mr Merriweather, but like everyone else around here, I've heard of him.'

'So, what are we going to do, Sheriff?' Jacob asked him bluntly.

Olsen rested his elbows on his desk and made an arch with his fingers. He didn't look Jacob in the eye. 'I need to think about this, Mr Merriweather. I need to think about it real hard.'

Jacob got up. 'See you in the morning,' he said, ' after you've had time to mull over the matter.'

They left the sheriff's office and untethered their horses.

'What do you think he'll do, Jacob?' Marie asked him.

Jacob grinned. 'He'll sleep on it and do nothing,' he said.

'Why do you say that?' she asked.

Jacob gave a sceptical chuckle. 'Because he's a liar, Marie.'

49

Marie was smiling. 'That's a bold accusation, Jacob!'

'I'm no mind reader, Marie, but I was watching that guy closely when I asked him what he was going to do and whether he knew Jack Davidson, and when he said "not personally" I knew he was lying, and that he knows Jack Davidson only too well. In fact I think they're close buddies.'

Marie looked surprised, but not unduly shocked. 'Maybe you're a better mind reader than you think,' she said. 'What will you do right now?'

He grinned. 'Well, Marie, I guess I must go back to my friend Sam Critchley and consult his great mind.' He paused. 'And what will you do?'

She gave him an arch smile. 'I think I should put a few chairs out and talk with those ladies who don't think I'm a witch.'

Jacob rode on, and before long encountered Sam Critchley, who was riding towards town in his painted wagon. Sam halted the burros and Jacob stopped alongside the wagon.

'Glad to see you're still in one piece,' Sam said.

'Well, I nearly had my scalp creased,' Jacob told him,

'How come?' the old man asked him.

Jacob told him all that had happened up at the cabin.

Sam grunted. 'That was pretty close, my friend, but I'm not totally surprised.'

'Did you ever meet Jack Davidson?' Jacob asked him.

'Oh, I met him right enough. He even came to one of my meetings and put a few dollars into the hat. He's a man you don't want to mess with. If you ever handled a rattlesnake you'll know what I mean. If that *hombre* gets his fangs into you, you'd better start to pray because there won't be much time left before you pad on, so to speak. You coming into town to hear my words of wisdom?'

Jacob smiled. 'I never miss a chance to improve my mind, sir.'

As they drew close to the striped tent they saw a whole host of people milling around, most of them womenfolk, though there was also quite a strong contingent of men. A few of them cheered, and some threw their hats in the air as the wagon approached. Obviously Sam's appearance was a matter of entertainment in a community where the only pastime, apart from hard work, was eating and making love, or having a singsong by the fire.

Sam went around shaking hands with folk and patting kids on the head. He was clearly extremely popular. Once again Jacob wondered whether he was an impostor or a genuine man of God.

Sam treated himself to a glass of fruit juice, and when the time came he climbed on to the dais and raised his hand, and the crowd became hushed. Jacob sat beside the tent facing the crowd, watching the faces. Most had eager and expectant expressions, but there were a few who looked less friendly; among them was a man dressed like a priest who scowled and mouthed his contempt at Sam. Marie sat in the front row. She had changed into her normal womanly clothes and she looked quite ladylike. As Jacob looked at her she smiled. 'She's a really fine woman,' Jacob said to himself.

Further back Sheriff Olsen stood slightly apart with his usual quirly hanging from his lip.

Old Sam Critchley certainly knew how to woo the crowd. He spoke eloquently and with conviction, and he soon had the audience in the palm of his hand. Jacob didn't listen to much of what he said. He was too intent on people watching, and at the back of the crowd he saw several hard-bitten characters who must have been ranch hands, who had probably ridden in for the entertainment or possibly to make trouble.

When Sam's oration came to an end, there was prolonged cheering and stamping of feet. But then Sam held up his hand for silence. 'Now, my friends,' he said solemnly, 'We all know about the cruel murder of Stan and Beth Salinger and I'm sure we want to see their murderers caught and brought before the law, Now I want you to take your minds back and if you can remember anything, anything at all, that will help Sheriff Olsen to track down those killers and bring them to justice, please come forward. The sooner we bring those killers to justice it will be better for everyone concerned.'

Now a large sombrero was passed round and folk were putting dollar bills and dime pieces into it. As usual some people were more generous than others. Jacob didn't take much note of that. He was watching the hard-bitten characters at the back of the crowd. He turned and saw young Hank the stable hand standing close beside him.

'Good evening, Hank,' Jacob said politely.

'Good evening, sir,' the boy crowed back.

'I wonder if you can help me, Hank?'

'It will be a pleasure, sir,' the boy said, no doubt remembering the generous tip Jacob had given him earlier

'You see those men standing at the back?'

'Sure thing, sir,' the boy said.

'Have you seen them before?'

The boy sort of giggled. 'Why, sure I've seen them, sir. They're ranch hands. They usually ride in after round-up when they get their pay and kick up a rumpus. They fire their guns into the air to put the scares on folk, but people lock their doors and nobody gets hurt.'

'Thank you, Hank. Buy yourself a drink and keep out of trouble.' Jacob handed him a dime.

The boy looked at him and grinned. 'Why, thank you, sir. Did you find a gold mine or something?'

Sam Critchley was on the bench of his painted wagon, still talking to his devotees. He looked down at Jacob and nodded, as if to say, 'Look where fame gets you, young man, but don't let it tempt you away from the truth.' What he actually said was, 'I'm going right back to my Happy Hunting Ground to camp for the night.'

Jacob tipped his Stetson. 'Maybe I'll join you later. Right now, I've got business to attend to.'

He walked into the Grand hotel where the three cow-punchers were already propping up the bar drinking their whiskey. He leaned on the bar and ordered a beer.

The bartender gave him a nod. 'So you're back again, Mr Merriweather.'

'Merriweather!' One of the cowpunchers turned to him. 'Haven't I heard that name somewhere before?' He was a big burly man who reminded Jacob of Black Bart somewhat.

'I guess you might have done,' Jacob said. 'But it isn't the usual run of names, is it?'

The big man turned to his *compadres*. 'You hear that, Wolf? This guy calls himself Merriweather.'

The man called Wolf grinned at Jacob. 'What kind of a name is that?'

Jacob put on his best smile. 'Name I was born with, my friend. So I have to carry it around with me until I die. Jacob Merriweather has to do for me. It's the only one I've got.'

'Until you die!' the burly man said with a grin. 'Well, let's hope that ain't any time soon. Mr Merriweather.'

'I share that hope,' Jacob said.

All three of the cowpunchers guffawed with laughter. Then the lean guy who hadn't spoken so far looked at Jacob along the bar. 'You from around here, Mr Merriweather?'

'Not so much,' Jacob said. 'I been all over.'

The burly waddy looked at his *compadres* and then at Jacob. 'You see a man on a chestnut-coloured horse with a sort of double blaze on its nose lately?'

'Well now, I do believe I have,' Jacob said. 'A tall guy with a mean face. In fact he took a couple of shots at me only yesterday morning.'

The three men exchanged suspicious glances.

'You wouldn't be fooling with us, would you, Mister?' the man called Wolf asked him.

'I don't fool with people, sir,' Jacob said. 'I saw the *hombre* you're talking about just a few miles from here. He took a couple of shots at me and I took a couple of shots back. Unfortunately he was on the move, and he vamoosed pretty quickly so I missed.'

The burly guy gave Jacob a wide grin that might have been almost friendly except for the eyes. 'Why don't I buy you a drink, *amigo?*'

'Well, it's been a long day and being shot at does give a man a thirst. So I'd be happy to accept your offer, my friend.'

They moved to a table and sat down, and the barman brought their drinks. Jacob ordered a beer since he couldn't stomach the whiskey the Grand hotel provided. As the barman placed his beer in front of Jacob he gave him a strange flicker of a smile. It was like a warning light flashing on and off.

'So the guy took a shot at you?' the burly man said.

'That's a fact,' Jacob agreed.

'And then the guy rode off,' the man called Wolf speculated. 'D'you mind if I ask you a couple of questions, Mr Merriweather?'

'Please ask away, sir, and if I can give you a good honest answer I'll be glad to oblige.'

Wolf gave a kind of grin that Jacob thought suited his name well. 'Did you see which way the *hombre* rode after you shot back at him?'

Jacob rubbed his chin thoughtfully. 'Well now, I guess that would be towards town.'

Wolf looked at his *compadres* and nodded. 'So he came this way?' he said.

'I guess so,' Jacob replied, 'but he might have branched off somewhere. All roads don't necessarily lead to Rome, do they?'

'That's true,' Wolf said with a look of enquiry. He obviously hadn't a clue about Rome.

The lean guy pointed a finger in Jacob's direction. 'And what were you doing up at the cabin, Mr Merriweather?' he asked.

'Escorting a friend of mine,' Jacob replied, 'and generally minding my own business.'

He felt the three cowpunchers stiffen. Then they looked at one another with deep suspicion. 'Are you fooling with us, Mr Merriweather?' the burly guy asked.

'Like I said,' Jacob replied, 'I don't fool with people. I tell things like they are.'

Wolf nodded slowly. 'I see you carry a gun, Mr Merriweather. Which suggests you're a gunfighter. Would that be right?'

Jacob paused for a moment. 'If I didn't carry a gun, sir, I'd be dead meat by now. I guess the guy on the chestnut horse with the unusual blaze would have been happy to kill me up at the cabin.'

The burly man scrutinized him closely. 'What are you doing in town, anyway, Mr Merriweather?'

'Mostly minding my own business,' Jacob said. 'There's nobody minds it as well as I do, in my experience.'

Wolf and the lean guy exchanged glances.

The lean guy said, 'Are you looking for work, Mr Merriweather?'

'I might be, and there again, I might not. Depends what the work involves. Had you anything particular in mind?'

'Did you ever hear of the Circle Bar Ranch?'

'Can't say I have, sir. Who runs it, anyway?'

The lean guy pulled a sceptical face. 'Biggest ranch in the territory. The boss man is Jack Davidson. The ranch has been in his family for three generations. I'm surprised you haven't heard of it.'

'Well, sir, if Mr Davidson made me an offer I might just accept it, depending on what it was. But as you probably see, I'm no waddy. I don't know which end of a cow is which. Which can be somewhat inconvenient'

The three cowhands laughed raucously. Then the lean guy said: 'It's not just handling cows, Mr Merriweather. There might be other possibilities.'

'Like what?' Jacob asked.

The lean guy shrugged. 'Why don't you ride up there sometime and find out?'

Jacob nodded. 'I might just do that. As soon as I'm through with my present business.'

Jacob shook hands with the cowhands and went out through the swing doors to the sidewalk. The striped tent and the dais had been removed and the last of the chairs were being cleared away. There was no sign of Sheriff Olsen or Marie. It's probably just as well, he thought; that lady with the sweet smile doesn't want to get tangled up in this mess, does she?

He thought of the three cowpunchers still sitting in the saloon, and a chill wind seemed to ruffle the hairs on the back of his neck. Then he unhitched his horse and mounted up and rode back to the place where Sam Critchley had parked the painted wagon.

Sam was sitting by the fire counting the dollar bills. He looked up and smiled. 'Well, you're still in the land of the living, I see.'

'Just about,' Jacob said.

He dismounted and led his horse down to the river where he let it drink and graze with Sam's burros. Then he squatted by the fire with Sam.

'Looks like you did well,' he said.

Sam stowed the dollar bills in a wooden box and put the box in a bag beside him. 'Those folk are real generous,' he said. 'This will keep me alive for a while.'

You old fraud! Jacob thought.

Sam looked at him and smiled. 'Every worker is worthy of his hire,' he said.

'You could be right,' Jacob agreed.

Sam was still smiling through his beard. 'Better to live by the word than live by the gun or the sword,' he said.

Jacob thought of those three cowhands drinking in the Grand hotel and he remembered the smile on their lips which didn't match the cold look in their eyes. He told Sam about the encounter. 'And one of them offered me a job at the Davidson ranch,' he said.

57

'You think you might take it?' Sam asked him.

Jacob was staring at the fire as though he could see his future in the flames. 'Be interesting to meet that guy,' he said.

'Well,' Sam said, 'Your tent's still here. So why don't you just bed down and sleep till sun-up, and then we can decide what to do about Davidson and his boys?'

'I think I'll just do that, my friend. It's been a long day and I'm just about tuckered out.'

He was dreaming about coffee and hot juicy steaks and the young woman with the beguiling smile when he woke suddenly. Had it been a voice or the sound of movement? He couldn't be sure. So he grabbed his gun and peered out and saw a man standing close by with a revolver trained on him.

'Put that gun down before I shoot you!' the man commanded.

Jacob lowered his gun and laid it beside him on the ground.

The man turned towards the painted wagon as Sam Critchley poked his head out. 'What's wrong?' Sam said. 'Can't a man get his sleep around here?'

'Get down from your perch and walk slowly to the fire,' the man said, moving the gun to cover him.

Sam climbed down from the wagon and approached the fire with his hands raised.

The man moved the gun to cover Jacob again. 'You, get over to the fire.'

Jacob moved to the fire.

'Now, set yourselves down,' the man commanded. 'And keep your hands where I can see them in case I have to blow your heads off.'

58

'No need for threats, sir,' Sam said. 'We are men of peace.'

The man gave a sceptical grin. 'Then, why does this *hombre* carry a gun?' he asked, pointing his gun at Jacob.

Jacob held up his hands. 'I'm just a passing stranger and I carry a gun in case somebody takes a shot at me.'

He and the man with the gun studied one another for several seconds.

'Why, you're the guy who took a shot at me earlier,' the gunman said.

'And you're the guy who tried to shoot me dead up at the Salinger place,' Jacob said, 'And I've been wondering why you were there and who you are.'

'And why you turned up here,' Sam added.

The man raised his gun and aimed it at Sam. 'I'm here because I need supplies.'

'That's a strange word,' Sam said quietly with a smile. 'What supplies do you require? Are you looking for money or for food? I've got food but I'm a little short on money.'

'I think you're lying,' the man said, 'but I'll take the food anyway.'

Sam nodded. 'Why don't you wait here and I'll dig out the grub?' He rose from the fire as if to move to the wagon.

'Now wait a minute!' the man shouted. 'You think I'm gonna wait here while you climb up into that wagon and bring out a gun?'

Sam nodded calmly. 'If you want food, sir, that's the only way you're going to get it, because that's where it is.'

The gunman considered for a moment, and then he pointed his gun at Jacob again, and Jacob saw that his hand was shaking. 'What I want you to do is get the food, and if you make one false move I'm gonna plug this guy right through the head. Is that clear?

Sam nodded. 'That's clear enough, sir.' He climbed up into the wagon, and the gunman trained his gun on Jacob.

Jacob looked at him and grinned, though he wasn't feeling as brave as he looked. A shaking hand can be a dangerous hand, and that gun might go off either deliberately or accidentally at any second. So keep talking, he thought.

'You're making a big mistake, my friend,' he said quietly.

'Is that so?' the gunman muttered between his teeth.

Jacob gave a slight nod. 'That is so.'

'Maybe you'd like to say why,' the man said.

Jacob looked him in the eye. 'You were up at the cabin looking at the graves of those unfortunate young people you killed.'

'I didn't kill anyone!' the man interjected.

Jacob shook his head. 'You were one of the hired killers. Even if you didn't pull the trigger, you were there when those two young innocent folk were killed. I don't know why you returned to the scene of the crime or what you were looking for there, but I guess you took your pay and decided to cut loose.'

'How do you know that?' the man asked.

Jacob grinned at him. 'Let's just say I can read it in your eyes, my friend.'

The gun wavered slightly.

Jacob said, 'You're no natural born killer, my friend. So you decided to leave the ranch and ride off and look for a better life.' Jacob shook his head. 'Unfortunately, the ranch owner Jack Davidson has a long arm and he sent out three evil-looking *hombres* to find you and kill you, before you spilled the beans.'

The man looked horrified. 'How do you know that?'

'One is a big guy and the other guy is called Wolf. I don't know who the third guy is, but he's tall and lean and looks exceedingly mean.'

The man began to look scared as though he was confronted by Satan himself. 'Well, I'll be damned!' he whispered.

'Here's your grub,' Sam said as he climbed down from the wagon.

The gunman turned his head, and that's when Jacob made his move.

CHAPTER FIVE

Jacob reached out and struck the man's gun with his hand. The gun fired and the bullet hit the cooking-pot and ricocheted into the fire, sending up a shower of sparks and ash. Jacob stood up and kicked the gunman in the face as hard as he could, and the man fell back against the ground. Jacob brought down his foot and pinned the man's wrist to the ground. Then he retrieved the gun and hurled it away.

The gunman gasped and rolled over and tried to get to his feet, but Jacob was agile and strong and he kicked the man in the face again. Then he reached for his own gun and cocked it.

'Don't shoot!' the man cried, stretching out his hands.

Jacob stood over him and trained his gun on his head. 'Is that what those good folk said to you up at the cabin,' he growled, 'just before you shot them dead?'

'I swear I didn't shoot them!' the man squealed. 'It was Wolf and Stringer that did it!'

'Wolf and Stringer,' Jacob said. 'Wolf and Stringer.'

'That was a pretty good move,' Sam said from beyond the fire. 'Didn't do that old cooking-pot of mine any favours, but I guess I can still use it. It's almost like you'd practised that move a dozen times.'

Jacob was still getting his breath back. 'You don't need much practice when you see a gun pointing at you, Mr Critchley. It just comes naturally.'

'Well, now, whatever your name is,' Sam said to the gunman, 'why don't you just sit up and eat your last supper while you can?'

The gunman propped himself up as best he could. Jacob saw that he had a black eye and a horribly swollen lip, and wondered whether he was in a fit state to eat anything at all.

'You mean you're gonna go ahead and let me eat?' the man gasped.

'Well, now,' Sam said. 'We're not savages here, you know. You want to eat, you just go ahead and eat, that's if you can still chew without choking yourself to death.'

'And just remember this,' Jacob warned him, 'if you make a fool move I might just have to put an end to your worthless life with the aid of this gun. And by the way, who is this guy Stringer you mentioned?'

The gunman didn't reply. He was too busy wolfing down his food. Sam had been generous and it was a highly nutritious stew.

Jacob looked at Sam and wondered what they could do with this unnamed gunman, when the answer came out of the blue in the form of three riders. They had turned off the trail and were jogging steadily towards them.

The gunman swung round in panic. 'My God!' he gasped, 'it's them!'

Jacob grabbed him by the collar and pulled him away from the fire. 'Get over to the wagon and take cover!' he said.

The gunman crawled away on his hands and knees and

tried to make himself invisible, which wasn't easy.

Jacob stood up and waited with his gun held close to his shoulder. Out of the corner of his eye he saw old Sam standing close by with the gunman's gun in his hand.

'Good evening, gentlemen,' Sam said calmly.

The riders rode close and drew rein.

'Good evening, Mr Critchley,' the big man replied. 'I thought I heard a shot.'

'Just a passing hunter,' Sam said.

Wolf laughed. 'I see you got a gun in your hand, Mr Critchley. Ain't that a little unusual for a man of peace like you?'

'Well, I guess it is,' Sam agreed. 'But I do shoot the odd jack rabbit, and it comes in handy for rattlesnakes, too.'

Wolf shifted his gaze to Jacob. 'Didn't figure to see you here, Mr Merriweather.'

Jacob grinned and tightened his grip on his gun. 'Didn't figure to be here, sir.'

The man called Stringer grinned back. 'Thought I saw a friend of ours sitting with you when we rode up. Now he's gone. Can you explain that, Mr Merriweather?'

'Well, I can't explain that, sir. Maybe it was a vision of some kind. Who knows?'

Wolf nodded. 'Like I said earlier, we have a close friend we'd like a word with.'

'And if I see him around I'll be sure to tell him that,' Jacob said.

The air seemed to vibrate with tension. Jacob could feel even old Sam stiffen.

The burly man growled like a grizzly bear. 'You like to drop that gun on the ground nice and easy?' he said.

Jacob grinned and his teeth gleamed in the light of the fire. 'Is that an order or a request?' he asked.

'Take it whichever way you like,' the burly man said, 'just as long as you do as I say.'

Jacob lowered the cocked gun and pointed it at the burly man, 'Why don't you just turn your horse and ride away?' he said quietly.

'Is that an order or a polite request?' Wolf said. And he and Stringer drew their guns.

'Take it whichever way you like,' Jacob said. He glanced at Sam and saw that Sam was still holding the gun.

'Now listen up, boys,' Sam said quietly. 'We don't want to get too excited here, do we? Why don't we. . . .' But he never had the chance to finish his sentence because at that moment two things happened: Jacob fired his gun and dived away to the left, and Stringer and the burly man fired their guns simultaneously.

For a long moment nothing happened, and then the burly guy's horse pranced to one side and the burly man slid from the saddle and fell to the ground. Then everything happened at once. Jacob was stretched on the ground firing as fast as he could. The horses were prancing and rearing, and Wolf and Stringer were firing wildly at Jacob. And Sam was running with surprising nimbleness and diving for cover.

Wolf and Stringer reined in their horses and then turned them towards the trail and galloped away.

Jacob crouched and ran forwards. The retreating gunmen turned and fired several times without effect, but Jacob knew that a man on a horse had a one-in-fifty chance of hitting his target, so he didn't waste bullets firing back.

He ran to where the burly guy was lying. The burly guy raised his head and gasped. 'You . . . you. . . .' he croaked. And then blood came bubbling from his mouth and he fell back dead.

'What a way to go!' Sam reflected.

'What a way to live!' Jacob said. He looked down at the gun Sam was still holding. 'Did you fire that thing, my friend?'

'Never fired a shot in my life,' the old man said.

Jacob looked towards the painted wagon. 'What happened to the guy you fed?'

'I don't know,' the old man said. 'He's probably half a mile away by now.'

'I don't think so.' Jacob went to the back of the wagon and peered through the darkness towards the river. He could just make out the silhouette of a man among the horses and burros. He ran on towards the river just as the man was about to mount one of the horses.

'You mount that horse and I'll take a pop at you!' Jacob shouted. 'I've already shot one man today and another won't make much difference.'

The man hesitated and then dropped back on to the ground.

'Now walk slowly towards me,' Jacob said.

The man moved forwards slowly with his hands up.

'That's good enough,' Jacob said. 'I've saved your worthless hide once already, but twice might be a little too much to expect.'

'So you killed the big man?' the man said.

Jacob shook his head. 'I didn't want to, but it was necessary to stop him and his buddies from killing you. And I would say it's a little ungrateful of you to turn tail like that.'

The man was now standing close beside him. 'So what will you do now?' he asked.

'Me and my friend Sam will need to think about that.

Just walk back to the wagon nice and easy, and we'll talk about our plans for your future, such as it is.'

They crouched by the fire. Sam's usual calm demeanour had returned. He looked at the prisoner and smiled. 'That was damned ungracious of you, boy,' he said to the prisoner. 'And since we're talking, maybe you could tell us your name. I'm always happier knowing a man's name. Numbers aren't quite the same, are they?'

The prisoner looked across at him with a puzzled frown. 'Name's Killop,' he said.

'Which is somewhat appropriate for a killer,' Sam speculated.

A look of defiance appeared on Killop's face. 'I tell you, I didn't kill those people!' he declared.

'Well, that's good,' Jacob said, 'because come sun-up, you're going to have the chance to prove it.'

'What do you mean?' Killop asked him. He obviously didn't know how to take these two weird *hombres* who talked so strangely.

'What I mean is this, my friend,' Jacob said. 'After we've all taken a good hearty breakfast we're going to ride into town and lock you up good and tight in the town jail so you can face the judge and give your evidence. And if what you say is true, you might have the chance to see Wolf and Stringer and your boss man swing from a tall tree for the crime.'

A look of horror appeared on Killop's face, which wasn't pretty at the best of times, and he gasped 'I can't do that! Those men will kill me first!'

'Well, my friend, I hope that's not true because you're our ace in the hole. So we'd better make sure you stay alive.'

*

Killop slept by the fire under Jacob's watchful eye. He could have made a break for it, but Jacob figured he had seen enough sense to keep quiet and sleep. Jacob stretched out behind the wheels of the wagon so that Killop couldn't see whether he was asleep or awake, and Sam slept in the wagon as usual.

As soon as the first glimpse of dawn began to show, Sam was up and about, rustling up the good hearty breakfast Jacob had promised. Jacob crawled out from under the wagon and prodded the sleeping Killop with his boot. 'Get your butt up, my friend. There's heavy work to be done.'

Killop peeped out from under the blanket Sam had provided. 'So, it's morning,' he said.

'I guess his majesty the sun would agree with you on that, and we must soon be on our way. But first you'd better take a leak and then you can help me with the horses.'

The horses had been hobbled, so if Killop had managed to mount up the evening before he wouldn't have got very far, anyway. After searching along the river bank they came across Stan Salinger's horse with its characteristic blaze, and close by, the dead man's horse.

Sam hitched the team of mules to his wagon, and they were ready to go.

'So, do I ride in the wagon?' Killop asked Jacob.

'What you do is you ride ahead of us on Stan's horse,' Jacob said. 'I guess that horse has got used to you by now. He might not like you a lot, but he'll be happy to carry you to hell and back if you ask him nicely. Horses are like that. They're very obliging creatures. You could say they're man's best friend, though some *hombres* would claim that honour for the dog.'

Jacob and Killop waved the flies away from the big

man's body and hoisted it across the back of his horse with some difficulty since he was as heavy as a whole stack of hay, though he didn't smell quite as sweet. Jacob then looped a lariat around Killop's body so he couldn't make a break for it, and ordered him to mount up. After that the whole cavalcade started towards town, with Killop leading the way with a rope attached to Jacob's saddle horn, followed by the dead man's horse with the corpse across its back, and then Sam on his wagon drawn by his burros.

It wasn't long before they came to the outskirts of town, and already the inhabitants were going about their daily business. Old Sam Critchley waved to the folk he knew, which was almost everyone.

'Hi there, Sam!' one man shouted. 'So you've come back with your healing hands.'

'Just bringing in the fruits of my labours with the help of my good friend Jacob Merriweather,' Sam replied cheerfully. 'You seen Sheriff Olsen this morning?'

'Not so far,' the man replied with a laugh. 'He likes the streets to have a good airing before he steps out.'

'Well, I hope he's had a good hearty breakfast because he's got an awful lot to do today,' Sam said.

The man looked at the body lying across the horse. 'Has there been a shooting, Sam?'

'Well, yes, some *hombres* took a pop at us. So my friend Jacob here had to shoot back, and unfortunately, this poor benighted guy was in the way of a bullet. So we've brought him in for respectable burial.'

Actually, the man had done Sheriff Olsen an injustice, because at that moment Olsen appeared at the door of his office with the first quirly of the day in his mouth. When he looked up and saw the cavalcade approaching, he opened his mouth wide and the quirly fell on the sidewalk.

'What the hell is this!' he exclaimed.

'This is an important delivery, Sheriff,' Jacob said. 'One dead man who tried to kill us, and one living gunman who tried to rob us. So I hope you've got room in your jail to lock a man up until the judge shows up, and then we can take this dead man to the funeral parlour so the director can do his business. Mr Critchley tells me he's quite an expert in putting the dead under the ground on Boot Hill.'

Sheriff Olsen stepped off the sidewalk and looked up at the body. 'Who is this?' he asked.

'Well,' Jacob said, 'I know he doesn't look too healthy at the moment, but he's one of the *hombres* who took a pop at us last night, and he's also one of Jack Davidson's ranch hands. If you look a little closer, I think you might recognize him.'

Olsen didn't bother to take up Jacob's offer. Instead he turned his attention to Killop, who was still sitting on Stan's horse, looking more than a little apprehensive. 'So what's with this *hombre*?' the sheriff asked.

'I'm surprised you don't recognize him, Sheriff, because he's one of Davidson's bunch too.'

Olsen looked baffled. This was uncharted territory, and he didn't quite know how to navigate it.

'So,' Jacob continued, 'I want you to lock up Mr Killop in the town jail and make sure he's safe and sound because he's a key witness in a trial for the death of those two innocent folk you found up at the Salinger place.'

'You can't lock me up in the jail!' Killop protested. 'I'd be a sitting duck in there.'

'Well,' Jacob said, 'I think you have to take your chance

70

of being roasted, but I don't think you need worry too much because Mr Olsen here is going to put you in the best cell in town and make sure you're fattened up in good time for the trial.' He looked at Olsen. 'Isn't that so, Sheriff?' he asked.

Olsen looked nonplussed. 'I need to take advice on that, Mr Merriweather.'

'Good idea,' Jacob said. 'Send the judge a wire – he'll know how to advise you.'

They locked Killop up in the town jail and took the body over to the funeral parlour. The funeral director looked at the body and exclaimed, 'Why, I know this man! I saw him in town only the other day. He's one of Jack Davidson's men. How was he killed?'

'Well, I myself had that pleasure,' Jacob replied. 'He was about to shoot me, but I managed to shoot him first. Otherwise you might have been putting me in the ground instead of him. So I have no regrets to speak of.'

Jacob stepped out of the funeral parlour and saw a crowd of townsfolk congregating round Sam Critlchey's wagon.

'What's happened?' 'Who got killed?' 'How did it happen?' they were asking.

Poor Sam was trying to keep calm in the face of this bombardment. He held up his hand and spoke, 'Good people,' he boomed out like an Old Testament prophet. 'There's nothing to worry about. Some men attacked us by the river and we managed to fight them off and, as you saw, one man got killed in the mêlée. And Sheriff Olsen has taken a man into custody. That's all I can say at the moment. Best to go back and attend to your business. No doubt you'll hear more about it later.'

'Who's the man in the town jail?' a man demanded.

'You'll have to talk to Sheriff Olsen about that,' Sam told him.

Jacob didn't pay much attention to this babble. His eyes were on a group of women at the back of the crowd, among them Marie Silversmith. She was staring at him with her keen inquisitive eyes. He threaded his way through the crowd until he reached her.

'I heard what happened,' she said. 'Thank God you're safe!' Her hand reached out towards him.

'I'm afraid I had to shoot a man,' he said, 'but the guy who took a shot at us up at Stan and Beth's cabin is in the town jail. His name's Killop.'

Marie smiled. 'Why don't you come to my place and sit down. You must be exhausted.' When she used the word *exhausted* Jacob realized he was indeed weary. Sleeping under Sam's wagon and keeping a weather eye on Killop hadn't been exactly conducive to sleep!

He went over and unhitched his horse and then Stan's horse.

Marie Silversmith's cabin was somewhat back from the main drag. Beside it there was a pasturage where Marie grazed her horse. Jacob released his own horse and Stan's, and Marie's horse looked up and neighed.

'A friendly greeting,' Marie said. 'That's a good sign.' She gave him an arch smile. 'Please come inside.'

'Well, Marie,' he said. 'I don't want to ruin your reputation.'

She raised an eyebrow. 'You don't need to worry about that, Jacob. I have no reputation to lose. As I told you, I'm thought of as a witch.'

They went inside and Jacob noted immediately how tidy the place was. 'So this is where the witch lives,' he said. 'I see no sign of a broomstick.'

'I find horseback more convenient,' she said. 'I don't care too much for heights. I get nervous even climbing the stairs.' She looked him full in the eye with those large, spellbinding eyes of hers. 'I've been worried about you, Jacob. You could have been shot.'

'Well, I was a little worried myself.' He looked straight back into her eyes and smiled.

She held his stare and moved closer. 'D'you mind if I ask you a personal question, Jacob?'

'Depends how personal it is,' he said quietly.

She breathed in slowly. 'It's probably the most personal question you've ever been asked.'

Jacob felt his heart beating so fast he could scarcely breathe. 'Please ask the question, Miss Silversmith.'

'Would you mind if I put a spell on you, Mr Merriweather?'

Jacob was smiling so much he thought his face would split and for a moment he couldn't speak. Then he said very quietly, 'You already have, Marie.' It was as though he had crossed a river and there was no going back. He stretched out his arms and she came straight to him, and for a long moment they stood together and their cheeks glowed with wholesome fire. And then they kissed, and their kiss lasted for a very long time.

Jacob felt like the sky had opened and a spirit had drawn him into heaven.

'So, is that how a witch kisses?' he murmured.

'I wouldn't know,' she gasped. 'It never happened that way before.'

'So what happens now?' she asked him.

'Well,' he said, 'It seems we have a lot of thinking to do.

73

You're a witch and I'm a gunman. Is that a good combination?'

'Speaking as a witch,' she said, 'I think it's what we want it to be. When I stir up the plum pudding at Christmas, the ingredients mix together fine and the result is delicious.'

'Well,' Jacob said. 'I always enjoy a good plum pudding.' He paused. 'But there's a difficulty here. . . .'

'There's always a way to get round a difficulty if you look hard enough,' she said. 'So what's the difficulty?'

They were both smiling and Jacob felt that however long they debated, the die was already cast. It was like wading into a fast-flowing stream and being swept away by the tide. And this tide was warm and friendly and seemed to flow on for ever.

'Well,' he said at last, 'the truth is, I've hardly got a bean to my name. I'm just a wandering tumbleweed blowing about in the wind.'

She nodded and smiled. 'Even tumbleweeds find a resting place sooner or later. It's part of the life cycle.'

Jacob shook his head. 'You sure have a lot of savvy for a witch.' He took her in his arms and they enjoyed another long, deep kiss, and were lifted right off the ground on to the tide of passion!

I could have ridden right on to Oregon where the apples grow all the year round, but I turned back and met Marie. Was that what some folk call Fate, or was it a coincidence? Jacob wondered.

They were now sitting opposite one another across the table. Marie had made them both drinks.

'So what do you see in your magic orb now?' he asked her.

She held her head on one side. 'I might be a witch, but

I can't look into the future. If we could look into the future we'd probably just die on the spot.'

'Which would not be a happy ending.'

She looked at him with her keen enquiring eyes. 'But,' she said. 'I could make a guess.'

'So what's your guess, Marie?'

She was looking at his hands resting on the top of the table. 'You have capable hands, Jacob, but they are also rash hands.'

'So what does that mean?'

She looked him in the eye again. 'It means that when you make up your mind to take a journey, you go all the way.'

He raised an eyebrow. 'So what does all the way mean?' he asked.

She gave a wry smile. 'I should have foreseen this when I asked you to escort me to Beth and Stan's cabin. When Killop took a shot at us something inside of you made up your mind for you.'

'Made up my mind to do what?' he asked.

'It was then you decided to go after the killers and bring them to justice,' she said.

He looked at her and nodded. 'I do believe you're right on that, Marie.'

'The question is, how do we bring Jack Davidson to justice?' she said.

'Did I hear you say "we"?' he asked.

She looked at him steadily for several seconds. 'That's because wherever you go, I'm going with you, Jacob.'

CHAPTER SIX

Jacob looked at Marie across the table, and now he wasn't smiling. 'I don't think I can let you do that.'

'Well, when I make up my mind there's no way anyone can stop me. So maybe I'm just as stubborn as you.' She shrugged her shoulders. 'And it might be useful to have a witch along. Men can be brave and sometimes reckless, but witches are better at planning and more cautious. And they have what some folk call *intuition*, too!'

Jacob looked thoughtful. 'And what does this witch's intuition tell her about Jack Davidson and his bunch of killers?'

'I'm afraid I can't answer that until I've put my witch's hat on,' she said.

'Can you shoot straight?'

'If needs be I can shoot as straight as any man, and probably better than most,' she declared. 'I've been deer hunting with my pa many years ago. But I've never shot a man, and never wanted to until now.'

'Killing a man is a hell of a lot harder than killing a deer,' Jacob told her. 'You can eat a deer, but you can't eat a man.'

'How many men have you shot, Jacob?' she asked.

'More than I care to mention,' he said, 'And it doesn't come any easier, despite what they say.'

Marie shook her head and smiled. 'You're a good man, Jacob.'

'If you think that, you don't know me as well as you think you do.'

'I know you well enough to trust you, Jacob. That's what my witch's intuition tells me.'

They left the house and walked towards Main Street, and met Sheriff Olsen.

'Ah, Mr Merriweather,' the sheriff said. 'I think it's time we had a real conversation.'

Jacob raised his hat. 'Well, I'll be happy to talk to you, Sheriff, just as long as you've got that killer locked up tight in the town jail.'

Olsen blinked. 'Are you sure he's a killer, Mr Merriweather?'

'Well, I'm as sure as hell he took a shot at me and Marie,' Merriweather affirmed, 'and I'm as sure as hell glad he missed. And another thing I'm sure about is, he's going to give evidence against the men who killed those good people Beth and Stan, and the man who paid them to commit those murders.'

'How can you be sure of that, Mr Merriweather?'

Jacob held his head on one side. 'Nothing's certain in this life, Sheriff, except life itself and death. We're lucky to be born, and we don't know when we're going to pass along, as the saying goes. Everything in between is in the mists of time, and I don't think you can see as far as that, even with your specs on.'

Sheriff Oson gave a sceptical grin. 'I think you should know, Mr Merriweather, I've been looking into your past and I know more about you than you may think.'

'Well, that's an education in itself,' Jacob agreed. 'So maybe you could tell me my life story. I'm sure you've enjoyed digging it up.'

Ollson nodded. 'I sent a wire through to River Fork and the sheriff there replied pretty quick. It seems you're wanted by the law down there. You rode with Black Bart and his bunch, and as you know, that ruthless killer has now paid the price with his neck.'

Jacob glanced at Marie. 'That's no secret, Sheriff, even from Black Bart himself, though I doubt whether he thinks about it much where he's gone. So what do you aim to do about it?'

Olsen blinked. 'I think I should take you into custody, Mr Merriweather.'

'And lock me up with Killop. I'm sure we'd get along just fine together. There's only one problem.'

'And what might that be?'

Jacob glanced at Marie again. 'That's because I aim to bring those killers to justice, and I mean to do it before I travel on, or die.' He shrugged. 'By the way, Sheriff, I heard a rumour the other day.'

'What was that?'

'That the big rancher Jack Davidson was once an acquaintance of yours.'

Olsen's eyes narrowed and he turned a shade paler. 'Who told you that, Mr Merriweather?'

Jacob shrugged again. 'You know how rumours spread. Someone starts a whisper and soon everyone in town hears it loud and clear.' He paused for half a second. 'But whether there's truth in that rumour, I'm not going to ask you. But I will strike a deal with you. After those killers have been brought to justice, I'll give myself up, and you can claim the reward, if there is one.'

'Why did you say that?' Marie asked as they were walking along Main Street.

Jacob smiled. 'Maybe it's because I'm a little high at the moment.'

'Well, you'd better pull yourself down to earth again,' she said, 'because Sheriff Olsen is a dangerous man, and if you cross him it's like plunging into a river in full flood and you're likely to be swept away and drowned.'

'Well, then, it's lucky I'm a pretty strong swimmer, isn't it?'

She shook her head and frowned. 'Are you ever serious, Jacob?'

'Well, I'm pretty serious about you.'

Marie looked at him with exasperation, but she was smiling too. 'You must realize that Jack Davidson will hear about what you said, and he'll be waiting for us.'

Jacob nodded. 'Well, that's a problem we have to solve. But right now I have a hunch that we should consult the oracle in the shape of Sam Critchley.'

Sam's painted wagon was sitting outside the Grand hotel and his burros were drinking at the horse trough. Jacob and Marie went inside through the swing doors and saw Sam perched on a stool at the bar. He was in deep conversation with the bartender. The bartender looked across at Jacob and Marie, and his usual stern features relaxed.

'Why, Mr Merriweather and Miss Silversmith, good to see you both again. What can I get you?'

'Well,' Jacob said, 'it sure won't be that hogwash you call whiskey.' He turned to Marie. 'Would you like a soda or a sarsparilla?'

'I think I'll have a beer,' she said.

Jacob ordered two beers, and he and Marie took them to the round table under the window. Sam finished talking to the bartender and came over and joined them at the table.

'Well, now,' he said with a smile, 'so you two have teamed up, I see.'

Jacob looked at Marie and smiled. 'And maybe you should be the first to congratulate us,' he said.

'I'd be happy to do that! When's the great day?'

Jacob reached for Marie's hand under the table. 'As soon as possible. Maybe you could do the honours?'

'Well, I'm just a wandering preacher and I'm not licensed for marriages or funerals,' Sam said. 'I think you should see the priest. He thinks I'm a witch doctor or something, but I'm told he does a good line in weddings, and he's a real expert in funerals too. But I don't think you're quite ready for that yet.' He was smiling mischievously behind his long white beard.

Sam looked at Jacob: 'What do you aim to do, my friend?'

'Are you a mind reader?' Jacob asked him.

'Pretty close,' the old man said. 'The human species is very complicated, but the brain sends out signals, and if a man's very patient, he can pick up on those signals and read them pretty well.' He turned to Marie. 'I guess you can do it too, Miss Silversmith. It just takes a bit of practice.'

Jacob leaned forwards. 'OK: tell me what I'm thinking.'

Sam creased his brow. 'Dangerous thoughts. You're thinking of going after Jack Davidson and bringing him to justice.' He held up an admonitory finger. 'Did you ever hear of that priest who stuck his head in a lion's mouth? It was somewhere in England not so long ago, I believe.'

'What happened?' Jacob asked.

Sam grinned, 'The lion bit his head right off, of course.'

Both Jacob and Marie looked at Sam in dismay.

'That was a damned foolish thing to do,' Marie said.

'Precisely,' Sam said. 'So, if we're going to get Jack Davidson we need to cook up some kind of plan.'

Jacob looked in the direction of the swing doors and saw a familiar figure standing just inside. The man gave him a wave of the hand and came over to the table.

'Good day to you,' he said.

'Good day to you, Running Deer,' Jacob replied.

Running Deer looked down at him and gave an enigmatic half smile. 'Saw you coming into the hotel and thought I ought to join you.' He spoke with an indefinable half-Indian accent

'Well, we're real glad to see you,' Sam said. 'Why don't you sit yourself down and have a drink?'

'Be glad to, sir.' Running Deer sat down at the table opposite Jacob.

Sam signalled to the bartender. 'A beer be OK?' he asked Running Deer.

'A beer will be just fine,' Running Deer said. He looked across at Jacob. 'There's something I have to say to you, Mr Merriweather.'

'I figured there must be.'

Running Deer nodded. 'I hear rumours,' he said gravely.

'What kind of rumours?' Jacob asked him.

Running Deer looked at him earnestly with his deep brown eyes. 'I know you shot the big man who's lying in the funeral parlour, and I know there's a guy locked in the

81

calaboose name of Killop.'

'I guess everyone in town must know that,' Jacob said.

'I guess they do, Mr Merriweather,' Running Deer agreed. He picked up his glass of beer and studied it as though it might give him a clue as to how to proceed. 'I also know you mean to bring the men who killed those two innocent people to book.'

'That's a reasonable conclusion, Mister Running Deer Johnson. What's new?'

Running Deer stared deep into Jacob's eyes and said abruptly, 'You can't do it!'

There was a long pause. Everyone seemed to stop breathing. It was so quiet Jacob heard the clock over the bar ticking as though it was about to toll the bell of doom.

Running Deer raised his glass and drank his beer down to the dregs. Then he placed his glass on the table and said, 'You can't do it without my help, sir.'

'Why not?' Jacob asked after a pause.

Running Deer gave him another straight look. 'Because you'll be dead before you get within a mile of the ranch.'

'So how can you help?' Sam asked.

Running Deer reached down and suddenly produced a pistol. Everyone froze, and Jacob tensed and threw himself to one side.

Running Deer said, 'That was quick, but not quick enough, Mr Merriweather. If I meant to kill you, you'd be lying with a hole in the head under the table right now.' He laid his gun on the table in front of him and raised both hands. 'That's the way it is with Jack Davidson. If he wants you dead, you're dead before you know it.'

'Have another beer, Running Deer,' Sam Critchley said with relief.

'Thank you, sir, I do believe I will.' Running Deer sat

back with his hands across his chest. Jacob reached out and picked up the gun. It was an old Navy cap and ball. 'This gun isn't loaded,' he said.

Running Deer grinned. 'That is so, Mr Merriweather, but it might have been.'

Sam smiled. 'You took a terrible risk on that, Running Deer. Mr Merriweather could have shot you dead.'

Running Deer nodded in agreement. 'That is true, Mr Critchley, but I wanted to show you something.'

'Show us what?' Jacob asked him.

'First, how easy it is to die when you're dealing with a *hombre* like Jack Davidson. You see, I know Davidson well because I used to work for him as a wrangler. I've always been good with horses, like my pa. He taught me everything I know.'

'So, how do you propose to help us?' Jacob asked him.

'Well, it's like this, Mr Merriweather,' Running Deer said. 'I feel right sore about those killings, and I also know how the man Davidson is, and he's a real mean son of a bitch. So, if you'll have me, I'd like to ride along with you because I know how that ugly bastard operates, and if I can help, you won't get yourselves into deep shit.' He turned to Marie. 'Beg pardon for the language, Miss, but no language is too strong when you're dealing with a man like Davidson.'

Marie smiled. 'So how can you help us, Running Deer?'

Running Deer looked at them one at a tine. Sam glanced at Jacob and Marie. 'I guess that will be three of us, Running Deer.'

Running Deer shook his head. 'That's impossible. An old man who never carries a gun, a lady who ought to be home looking after the house and the chickens, pardon me saying so, Miss Marie, and a man who's good with a gun but doesn't know the territory. It doesn't fit.'

'Well, I'm going to be part of the outfit, whatever you say,' Marie affirmed. 'I can shoot as well as any man.'

Running Deer pulled a sceptical face. 'Well, Miss Marie, you might shoot a jack rabbit or a coyote, but shooting a man is another thing altogether. My woman Sophie is pretty tough, but she couldn't shoot a man . . . even if it happened to be me,' he added with a wry grin.

Merriweather was nodding and thinking. Could this half-breed Indian be trusted? Running Deer looked at him and seemed to read his thoughts. 'You are wondering what's in this for me,' he said. 'The answer, Mr Merriweather, is justice. That's what I believe in.'

Jacob looked at Marie and she nodded and smiled as if to say, 'I can read this man, and he's telling you the truth.'

Jacob looked towards the bar and saw that the barman was well out of earshot and minding his own business. Can we trust anyone in this town? he wondered. He knew that Sheriff Olsen must already know the four of them were meeting in the Grand hotel bar. Maybe he should have ridden on to Oregon after all. But then he looked at Marie and knew why he had to stay and see this thing through to the end.

'So,' he said quietly, 'how can we go about this business, Running Deer?'

Running Deer spread his hands on the table. 'Well, one thing's for sure, we don't just head out together and aim at the Davidson spread. When I leave here, I'll go home and saddle up my best horse.' He looked at Sam. 'And if you're intent on coming, Mr Critchley, I suggest you leave your rig somewhere here where it's out of sight. My wife Sophie will be happy to look after the burros and the rig, and you can ride your best burro. Leave after dark so you

84

don't attract too much attention. And you, Marie and Mr Merriweather can ride together earlier or later. it won't matter a damn as long as you don't attract attention.'

'What about you?' Sam asked him.

'I'll meet you at Stump Hollow some time tomorrow,' Running Deer said. He looked at Marie. 'I guess you know Stump Hollow, Miss Silversmith?'

Marie nodded. 'I know it. It used to be a mine. There's an old deserted shack up there.'

Running Deer nodded. 'That's where I'll meet you. Can't say exactly when, but it will be sometime tomorrow.' He turned to Sam. 'You know the place, Mr Critchley?'

'Can't say I do,' Sam said.

Running Deer nodded. 'I've drawn you a map, sir.' He placed a scrap of paper on the table and Sam leaned forward and scrutinized it with one eye closed.

'Stow it away and don't let anyone else see it, sir,' Running Deer said. He got up from the table. 'Well then, I'll just slip away and see you later.' He patted the bulge where the cap and ball was concealed. 'And next time I see you this here old timer here will be good and loaded and ready for action – but don't shoot me by mistake.' He gave a lopsided grin and left as quietly as he had come. The bartender was so busy with his customers that he scarcely noticed.

'Well,' Sam said, 'that is some Indian. Moves like a shadow even indoors.'

Sam Critchley went over to the bar, and soon he and the bartender were engaged in deep conversation about all things under the sun. The bartender was nodding and smiling politely, trying to show interest in subjects he neither understood nor cared about.

Jacob and Marie went out through the swing doors and

Jacob looked up and down Main Street, but there was no sign of Sheriff Olsen. 'I just hope that Killop guy is still safe and tidy in the town caboose,' he said to Marie.

Marie was looking in the direction of the sheriff's office. 'That's not what I'm worried about, Jacob. The question in my mind is, has Olsen sent a wire through to the judge.'

They went back to Marie's cabin and gathered supplies for the trip. Then Marie put plates on the table and served up a meal. 'We're going to need food in our bellies,' she said. 'My intuition tells me we've got a rough time ahead.'

Jacob tucked into the meal with relish, 'Do you always cook like this?' he asked.

She smiled at her plate. 'Only on special occasions, Mr Merriweather.'

He smiled. 'Well, when we're together full time, Miss Silversmith, I hope every day will be a special day.'

'We'll make sure it is, Mr Merriweather,' she said. 'We'll make sure it is.'

After the meal Jacob checked his Colt Peacemaker and the Winchester, and made sure he had a good supply of shells. 'What about you?' he asked Marie. 'What will you have in your saddle holster?'

'I have my pa's old Springfield,' she said. 'I used it for deer hunting and it's as good as ever it was.'

'Well, I hope you don't have to use it,' he said, 'because it's a one-shot rifle. So every shot has to count.'

'Then it's a good thing I've got a steady hand and a good eye,' she said.

They sat and talked until the sun went down. Then they went out and saddled the horses. While they were in the pasture, Running Deer's wife Sophie suddenly appeared.

'Don't you worry about a thing, Miss Silversmith,' she said. 'I'll look after the horses while you're out yonder, and if you'll leave the key with me I'll look in on the house and make sure everything's in apple pie order. That's if you trust me.'

'Why, sure I trust you,' Marie said, 'and thank you for the kind offer.'

Sophie looked at Jacob and marvelled. 'You sure are tall, Mr Merriweather.'

'Well, thank you, Mrs Running Deer. I didn't do anything to deserve it. It's just the way I grew.'

'Well, the Great Spirit sure did a good job on you, sir.' She moved closer to Jacob and looked up at him as though he was the Leaning Tower of Pisa. 'Why are you taking Miss Silversmith on this crazy mission, sir?"

Jacob shook his head. 'I'm not taking her,' he said. 'She's taking herself. It's no use arguing with a determined woman.'

'Well, you take good care of her, sir, you hear me!'

Jacob looked at her and smiled. She was a woman of some spirit, and he wondered how she and her husband had managed to accommodate to the white man's world. It must have a taken a lot of grit. 'Don't you worry yourself, Mrs Running Deer. Everything's going to be fine. I feel it in my bones.'

It was getting on for midnight and most honest folk were in bed, but there were a few people lounging around on the sidewalk, and one man, high on booze, was singing some kind of hillbilly in an untuneful, high-pitched voice.

Jacob and Marie went out by the back way, avoiding the main drag. They would hit the trail half a mile or more beyond the edge of town, passing the odd homestead where the good folk were mostly snoring in their beds. It seemed Sophie's Great Spirit was looking down on them with favour because the moon soon peered between the trees to smile at them and light their way.

'So you know this old deserted mine really well?' Jacob asked Marie.

Marie nodded. 'Been there a few times.' Her teeth gleamed in a smile. 'No home comforts, as I recall. Just dust and spiders and maybe a rat or two. Bats as well, so I'm told, but nothing to suck your blood. No snug corners to sleep in, either.'

They continued along the trail for some distance. And then Marie drew rein and stopped. 'Funny how different things look at night,' she said.

'You sure you remember the way?' he asked.

'Don't worry,' she assured him. 'If we get lost at least we'll be together, in which case, I can cast a spell.'

Almost as if in response a coyote suddenly howled from a thicket close by.

'Well, they seem to know you're here,' Jacob said.

'Those critters know a whole lot more than you think.'

He followed her along a faint trail for quite a long way until he saw a grey shape looming up in front of them.

'This is it,' she declared with apparent relief. She dismounted and walked her horse forward. 'Plenty of grass for the horses to chew on.'

'Stay here,' Jacob said. 'I think I'd better check there's no one around.' He dismounted and walked towards the grey building. Fortunately, the moon held up a candle to show him the way. He felt like a knight approaching a dark tower. 'How the hell is Sam going to find his way here?' he asked himself.

The door had been cut down for firewood long before,

and inside it was creepy and weird. Suddenly a bat flew from the interior, brushing his face with its wings.

'Don't go in there,' Marie warned him.

'What do we do now?' Jacob asked her.

'We spread out our bedrolls and try to get some sleep. In the morning we'll need to be good and alert and ready for anything that might come our way.'

CHAPTER SEVEN

As was his custom, Jacob lay with his head on his saddle and his Colt Peacemaker within easy reach. He stared up at the stars but avoided the moon, since folk said that if you stared too long at the moon you got moon madness. He didn't believe that nonsense, of course, but he turned his head and looked at Marie's sleeping head. She was so close he could have touched her, but she was wrapped up in her bedroll and he heard her breathing steadily and knew she was already fast asleep.

'Is this me lying here under stars so close to a girl that I could touch her, or is it somebody else?' he asked himself. But before the answer came he was dreaming.

In his dream he was lying so close to a creek that, if he turned on his side he would roll off the bank and be swept away in the current and lost for ever. Then he woke with a start and saw a man standing with a gun pointing at his head. He reached for his Peacemaker but it would have been too late.

'So you see,' the man said quietly, 'always hold yourself ready, even when you're asleep. I fear you've got a lot to learn, amigo, and you'd better learn fast because you only have one life to lose, and out here it could be snuffed out just like a candle flame.'

Jacob sat up and blinked. 'How did you get here, Running Deer?'

'The usual way,' Running Deer said. 'You might be OK in town but you have to learn to tread lightly here!' He crouched down beside Jacob. 'That's what my people have learned from generation to generation. It's come to be part of our nature.'

'Where will you sleep, my friend?' Jacob asked him. Running Deer's teeth gleamed in the darkness, and he shrugged his shoulders.

'Don't you worry about me, Mr Merriweather. I just hunker down anywhere I find myself and sleep like a bat in a cave – but as soon as a mouse moves I'm as awake as though I'd never slept. Just the way the dumb beasts are. So they're not so dumb after all.' He straightened up and holstered his gun. 'See you in the morning, Mr Merriweather.' And then he disappeared as silently as he had come.

Jacob lay down again and tried to sleep.

Come sun-up he woke with the scent of wood smoke in his nostrils. He sat up and stretched his legs.

'Good morning, Jacob,' a voice said from close beside him. 'Did you manage to sleep?'

'On and off,' he said.

'Mostly off,' Marie laughed. 'When I looked over at you, you were snoring like a buffalo. Which was a pity, because it was so cold in the night I hoped you might crawl in with me so we could keep each other warm.'

'That's a promise we'll have to catch up on later,' he said. 'Right now I can smell wood smoke and when Running Deer is around that must mean breakfast.'

91

Marie got out of her bedroll and shook herself. 'I guess I'll go down to that creek and freshen up.'

Jacob watched her as she walked off in the direction of the creek. She was dressed in range clothes just like a man, but the way she moved told Jacob she was all woman to the core of her being.

Running Deer was bending over a pot by a fire he had built up close to the old mine. By daylight the building had lost its romantic charm: it was just a grey, derelict hulk that had seen much better days. In fact it had been a failed enterprise that had never been good to anybody. Jacob learned later that the owner had lost all his money and shot himself through the head.

Marie's idea of freshening up had been to shed her clothes and immerse herself in the freezing cold water. When she came out she looked at Jacob and laughed, 'Why don't you jump in?' she challenged. 'It's the best way to wake up after a rough night.'

'Because I'm a martyr to goose pimples,' Jacob replied. Nevertheless he rose to the challenge and plunged in – and decided that if Marie could stand that freezing water, she must indeed be a witch!

They sat around Running Deer's fire and felt the heat coming off it and seeping into their bones. Running Deer dished out the food, which tasted like manna from heaven!

'I wonder where Old Sam pitched up?' Jacob asked Running Deer.

Running Deer shrugged fatalistically. 'I think we have to be patient, Mr Merriweather. He'll be here soon enough.'

'Soon enough' turned out to be around midday. Sam rode in on his burro and sang out, 'It's me, Sam Critchley, so don't shoot in case you get the wrong man! And I don't want to die young. I don't think Saint Peter and the angels are ready for me right now. They're awful particular up there.'

Then he appeared between the trees riding his burro.

'What kept you?' Jacob asked him.

'Circumstances,' the old man replied.

'What circumstances?'

'Like avoiding action,' Sam said. He got down from his burro. 'When I rode out of town I had the distinct impression someone was tailing me.'

'Did you see anyone?' Running Deer asked him.

'No, I didn't see a human soul. It was just a creepy feeling I had. Call it premonition if you like.'

Running Deer looked up, suddenly alert and wary. 'Well, folks, we have to get out of here pronto because if Mr Critchley has been followed, it means we're in danger.'

No one argued with that. Jacob said, 'Marie, you and Sam go down to the creek, saddle up the horses and take cover among the trees. And don't show yourselves till I come looking for you. And Marie, hold that Springfield rifle of yours ready 'cause I think you might need it.'

Sam and Marie moved as quickly and as silently as they could down to the river. Jacob scooped up the bedrolls and his saddle and made for a thicket close to the deserted mine. Running Deer left the fire and his cooking pot and just faded away like a ghost into the thicket. A moment later he appeared beside Jacob.

'Hold your breath and keep as still as that mouse I mentioned,' he said quietly.

Jacob crouched down and held his Colt Peacemaker ready. 'I just hope Marie doesn't have to use that damned Springfield rifle,' he muttered to himself. 'That one-shot rifle is about as good as nothing against killers like Wolf or Stringer.'

They waited for what seemed an eternity, and Running Deer was so still he might have been a stone statue. Then he turned slowly towards Jacob and whispered, 'I hear them coming. So hold yourself ready so they don't see us, and don't shoot unless we need to.'

Jacob nodded, and wondered what 'need' meant! Then he heard the sound of horses approaching. They were moving steadily and slowly towards the ruined mine. He peered out and saw two riders approaching. They were now so close he could have taken a shot at them, but he kept himself still and slowed his breath. He could feel his heart pounding in his chest.

The riders rode right up to the fire and one of them dismounted. He had a quirly stuck in his mouth and Jacob recognized him as Sheriff Olsen. The other guy stayed in the saddle and Jacob saw it was the man called Wolf.

Olsen looked down at the fire and said, 'Well, looky here. This fire's still smouldering and this is the cooking pot they must have used. So they can't be far.'

Wolf was looking round holding his gun in readiness. He seemed to stare right through the thicket where Jacob and Running Deer were crouching. Then he turned towards the derelict mine. 'They might be in the building. Maybe I should take a looksee.'

He got down from his horse and moved towards the entrance. He turned towards Olsen. 'Cover my back while I go inside.'

He approached the doorway and fired a shot. The sudden explosion echoed through the empty building like a crack of thunder on a still day. 'Anybody in there come out before I come in and get you!' Wolf shouted. Then he disappeared inside and they could hear his spurs jingling.

Sheriff Olsen grabbed his horse's reins and jigged it round so it shielded him from whoever might be approaching.

'What do we do now?' Jacob whispered to Running Deer.

'We wait,' Running Deer mouthed at him.

Wolf emerged from the ruin, holding his gun. He approached the fire and looked into the cooking pot.

'Why, I do believe we almost caught them at breakfast,' he said, 'so they must be quite close unless they heard us and galloped off hell for leather.' He laughed, and Jacob had the impression he was drunk or high on some drug.

Olsen was a good deal more cautious than Wolf. He stood behind his horse and peered over its back from the ruin in the direction of the creek.

'I figure they're not far,' he said. 'They could even be watching us right now.'

Wolf growled like the wolf he was. 'Well, that old so-called spirit healer won't get far. He talks good, but he don't know his ass from his elbow. Don't even know when he's being tailed.'

Well, he got that wrong, Jacob thought. Old Sam's got more savvy in his little finger than Wolf's got in his whole damned body! The picture that came into his mind was so absurd he almost laughed. But then he froze.

'What do we do now?' Olsen asked Wolf.

'What we do now is we ride after them and put them in the land of the big sleep,' Wolf said. 'That's what the boss wants, and that's what the boss is gonna get.'

'After what you've been drinking, d'you think you can aim straight?' Olsen asked Wolf. Jacob thought he sounded somewhat nervous, as though he didn't care for this mission or Wolf one little bit.

Wolf gave a quiet chuckle. 'You don't need to worry none about that, Olsen. I shoot a lot better when I've had a few drinks. I see two targets and that gives me two choices.' He raised his gun and aimed into the bushes and said, 'Pop, pop, that's the way the shooter jumps, and they never know what's hit them.'

Jacob knew it was time to act, but as he rose and levelled his gun, Running Deer put a hand on his arm to restrain him.

Olsen mounted his horse and both men rode away towards the creek.

'Why did you do that?' Jacob demanded angrily.

For the first time Running Deer looked confused. 'Because killing's too easy, I want to see Wolf swing.'

'What about Marie and Sam?' Jacob asked him.

'Follow me!' Running Deer said.

Then Jacob discovered how Running Deer had acquired his name, because he ran so fast that Jacob couldn't keep pace with him. But Running Deer didn't follow the tracks to the creek. He cut away to the right and sprinted to the top of a low bluff from where he could look down and see the two riders.

Olsen and Wolf had stopped and dismounted, and Olsen was kneeling close to the creek and reading the signs. From where they were standing, Jacob and Running Deer couldn't hear what was said but Jacob judged by their body language.

'Lookee here,' Wolf said. 'This is where they picked up the horses and this is the way they went along the creek. If we ride on we can catch up on them and then take a pop at them. So follow me, Sheriff.'

Both men mounted their horses and rode beside the

creek, following the tracks of the horses.

'What the hell are we going to do without our horses?' Jacob asked Running Deer. 'Marie and Sam will be like sitting ducks.'

'Well, we'll just have to run like hell!' Running Deer said, and he started off in hot pursuit.

Once again Jacob was amazed at his speed and fitness. Running Deer continued along the bluff until he reached another vantage point where he stopped. Jacob stopped beside him and they both looked down towards the creek where Olsen and Wolf had reined in their horses. Jacob and Running Deer's horses were grazing beside the creek and there was a small stand of willows close by on a slight rise.

'No use shooting from here!' Running Deer said, catching his breath. 'Like shooting flies in a shooting gallery.'

But Jacob wasn't listening, he was thinking of Marie's desperate plight among those willows. He ran full tilt down the hill, and as he ran he heard Wolf shouting, 'Come out and face the music! You have a date with hell today.'

'Don't shoot!' Old Sam shouted from the willows. 'There's just me and Marie in here.'

'Well, that means two bullets!' Wolf laughed, and then he fired towards the stand of willows.

Jacob was half way towards the creek when he opened fire, but he was panting so hard he knew he had little chance of hitting anyone. Running Deer fired from above, but he was too far from his target to hit it.

Olsen looked up and jigged his horse round and fired in Jacob's direction but the bullet hissed in the grass just short of Jacob's feet. He heard Wolf laughing. Then Wolf fired two more shots into the stand of willows.

Jacob continued running down the hill with his gun held high. He was about to fire at Wolf again when there a single shot from the willows. Wolf jerked back in the saddle and keeled over and plunged to the ground. As he'd said himself earlier, 'They'll never know what hit them.'

Olsen swung round and fired a shot at Running Deer, but Running Deer was far to wary to be hit. He had already leapt sideways behind a bush and the shot went wide. Jacob aimed at Olsen and was about to open fire when Olsen held up his arms in surrender – but he still had his gun in his hand.

'Drop that gun!' Jacob shouted.

Olsen looked from Jacob to Running Deer and realized he had no choice, so he let the gun fall to the ground. Jacob ran forwards and kicked the gun into the long grass.

Running Deer stooped and picked up the gun and stuck it through his belt. 'You're lucky to be alive, Sheriff,' he said.

'You can't shoot me, Running Deer,' Olsen said. 'I'm an officer of the law.' Jacob saw beads of sweat breaking out like goose pimples all over his forehead.

'You're a disgrace to your office!' Jacob shouted in his face, 'and you don't deserve to be alive. Now sit down there and keep yourself still in case we have to shoot you, which might be a good idea, anyway.'

Olsen plonked himself down and looked as pale as parchment. 'You mind if I roll myself a quirly?' he asked timorously.

'Go ahead and smoke. There's plenty of smoke and fire where you're going to,' Jacob said. He turned to the willows as Marie emerged, supported by Sam who was trailing the Springfield in his left hand. Marie was sobbing as she looked down at Wolf's body, stark still in death.

'I killed a man!' she gasped.

'Well, my dear,' Sam soothed, 'you had no choice. Without that shot we'd both be dead.'

She turned trembling and saw Jacob, and rushed forwards into his arms. 'Jacob, I killed a man!'

Jacob put his arms around her and gave her a tender hug. 'You did what you had to do. I should have been there for you, but thank the Lord you survived.'

He kissed her on the forehead and felt her relax in his arms.

Jacob prodded Olsen with his Peacemaker. 'Get up on your feet!' he said.

Olsen was so wobbly that Running Deer had to help him to his feet. 'What are you going to do?' Olsen asked. 'Are you gonna shoot me?'

It was Sam who answered. 'We aren't barbarians, Mr Olsen. We don't shoot men. We hand them over so the law can decide. Right now we aim to take you with us wherever we go.'

'And right now we need to pick up our horses and gather our thoughts,' Jacob added. 'But I must warn you, Olsen, if you make a stupid move I shall have no hesitation in shooting you down like the cur you are, and you can kiss good-bye to that badge on your chest because after this I don't think you'll be needing it.'

Sam looked down at Wolf's body. It lay still with a look of astonishment on its not very pretty face. 'What do we do with the body?' he asked.

Jacob looked at it. 'In my opinion we leave it here for the buzzards and the coyotes. They'll be glad to oblige, and they never did anyone any harm.'

Running Deer nodded in agreement. 'And we can't

hang on here in case Davidson's men come down on us. So far we've been lucky, but we can't be too careful, can we?'

Sam shook his head. 'So if we can't give him a Christian burial we could say a prayer over his body. After all, he might have started good and then turned bad.'

'Like an apple rotting in an orchard,' Running Deer said. Then he turned and urged Olsen forwards towards the ruined mine.

'Now,' he said to Olsen, 'plant your ass down there by the fire and smoke to your heart's content because we've got a lot of talking to do. And remember this: I'll be more than happy to blow your head off if needs be. In fact it would give me a great deal of pleasure.'

Running Deer threw an armful of dry twigs on the fire and it sparked up almost immediately. It was cosy sitting there, and even Olsen started to relax as he smoked.

Old Sam sat on a bench and Running Deer squatted on his haunches facing the sheriff. Marie sat beside Sam, looking down at the Springfield rifle as though it were a poisonous snake. Sam put a comforting arm round her shoulders and said, 'You want to go back to town I'll be happy to escort you, Miss Marie.'

Marie looked up abruptly with defiance. 'No, Mr Critchley. Thank you, but no. I'm staying on right here.' She looked across at Jacob and smiled. 'I promised I'd bring those killers to justice and I mean to do it.'

She pointed at the Springfield. 'And if I have to use that thing again, I'll do it.'

Sam nodded benignly like Santa Claus. 'Well, you are indeed a very brave young woman, Marie, and that's a fact.'

Jacob and Running Deer smiled and nodded, and even

Olsen gave a smirk.

'Well then,' Jacob said to Olsen. 'So, tell me how you came to be a buddy of this guy Davidson?'

Olsen threw the stub of his quirly on the fire and rolled another. He looked at the smoke rising from the fire as though he hoped it might help him to see the future, and he didn't care too much what he saw. Then he took a deep breath. 'I've known Jack Davidson for a very long time,' he said.

'Exactly how long?' Jacob asked him.

'I knew his pa when the ranch was still a going concern. Mr Davidson senior was a fine man. In fact I worked for him way back. And I knew Jack Davidson when he was just a kid.'

Jacob nodded. 'And were you aware Jack Davidson planned to kill those two innocent young people at the farmstead just before I met you that time?'

Olsen looked deeply shocked. 'I swear to God I didn't know that!'

'God isn't too keen on lies, Mr Olsen,' Sam put in. 'He's too busy inventing the truth.'

'So,' Jacob said, 'why were you riding with the man who called himself Wolf, who happens to be lying waiting by the creek up there for the coyotes to pick over his bones?'

Olsen shook his head and avoided making eye contact.

Jacob grinned. 'Let me make a suggestion, Olsen. That guy Wolf came to seek you out so you could follow Sam here and do Davidson's dirty work for him.'

Olsen made no reply.

Jacob said, 'Isn't that the truth, Sheriff Olsen?'

Olsen shook his head. 'You don't know Jack Davidson. He's as friendly as pie on the outside, but if you cross him he's like the very devil himself.' As he spoke his lower lip began to tremble.

Jacob gave a wry grin. 'Well, we're going to get the chance to get acquainted with him quite soon, Sheriff, and you're going to have the pleasure of introducing us.'

Once again Olsen's lower lip trembled, and it was by no means a pretty sight. 'I can't do that,' he mumbled.

'Well, I wouldn't say you have much choice because we're going to walk right up to his door and you're going to arrest him and then we're going to take him back to town and put him on trial for murder.' Jacob pulled a sceptical face. 'And who knows, Sheriff, if you come out of this passing fair, you might even earn a medal, though I wouldn't place bets on that. And by the way, if we happen to meet Stringer on the way you'd better get ready to duck your head down before he gets what's coming to him.'

It was getting towards sunset so they decided to camp for the night. Running Deer had a way with fires, and soon he had one roaring away and throwing out enough heat to roast an ox. Between them Running Deer and Sam managed to make a really tasty supper, and even Olsen wasn't too squeamish about it. As they ate he looked across at Jacob. 'There's something on my mind,' he said quietly.

'Is this confession time?' Jacob asked him.

Olsen shook his head. 'It's my wife. She'll be wondering why I haven't come home.'

Jacob grinned. 'Like the lost sheep,' he said. 'Well, that's a real pity, Olsen, and I'm sorry we have to disappoint your good lady. And she must indeed be good to put up with a bastard like you. But fate is fate and you'll either show up late or show up dead, and there isn't a damned thing we can do about that.'

After supper Running Deer tied Olsen's hands behind his back. Olsen said, 'What happens if I need to take a leak in the night?'

'Well, now,' Jacob said, 'Mr Running Deer here is going to take you down to the creek and you can leak and dump as much you like.'

Running Deer grunted with laughter and led Olsen at gunpoint down to the creek.

Marie said, 'You're a hard man, Jacob.'

'You need to be hard with a guy like Olsen. Give him an inch and he'll take a mile even if it means shooting you dead. I'm just surprised he's lasted so long as sheriff. But I guess there have to be other crooked sheriffs in the West, and maybe in the East as well. The world is full of political criminals. You could say it goes with the job.'

Running Deer and Olsen came back from the creek. Then they all settled down in their bedrolls and tried to sleep. If they had been alone Jacob would have snuggled down with Marie, but at least it was warmer than the night before. Running Deer had built up the fire so that it would keep them warm all night. Like all First Nation people he was a dab hand with fires.

'Don't you worry none,' he said. 'Sleep easy and I'll keep the fire going through the night.'

Jacob lay on his back, thinking about the future, and before he finally started to sleep he heard the wail of the coyotes close to the creek.

CHAPTER EIGHT

As before, Running Deer cooked up breakfast. It wasn't much but it was enough. The sun rose like a poached egg in a grey pan, heralding an uncertain day.

Running Deer untied Olsen's wrists and took him down to the creek to freshen up. The sheriff made no complaint. If he attempted to escape it was a choice between drowning in the creek or being shot, neither of which appealed to him greatly. He was glad to get back to the warmth of the fire.

'Well, it looks like you've cleaned up well, Sheriff,' Jacob said. 'Why don't you just squat down here and take some breakfast. It's going to be a long day.'

Olsen gave him a quizzical look: most of the time he had no idea what Jacob was talking about. 'What d'you aim to do?' he asked.

Jacob smiled. 'Just like I said, Sheriff, you're going to have the pleasure of introducing us to your friend Jack Davidson.'

'How d'you figure that?' Olsen asked.

'Well, you could walk right up to the ranch house door and flash your badge at him and say, "Good day, Jack. Would you mind saddling up your horse and riding back to town because I'm arresting you for the murder of those two innocent young people back at the farmstead".'

Olsen looked at Jacob with widening eyes. 'You expect me to do it just like that?'

Jacob nodded. 'You do it any way you like, Olsen. It doesn't make a whole lot of difference to me as long as you get the message across. After all, you've lived most of your life in pretend land. So you shouldn't have too much trouble, especially when it comes to saving your own skin.'

Olsen gritted his teeth and stared at the fire.

After the meal Running Deer threw sand on the fire, and he and Jacob had a quick consultation.

'Well, now, Mr Merriweather,' Running Deer said, 'you talk like a lawyer but can you act like a soldier? Have you really planned this thing through?'

Jacob gave him a quizzical look. 'Well, I'll be straight with you, Running Deer. I'm a little uneasy about this whole procedure. There are only two soldiers in this outfit – you and me. Sam never carries a gun, and Marie finds it hard to shoot at bad men. So I would be a good deal happier if they went back to town and prepared a home-coming for conquering heroes, but that's not going to happen, is it?'

Running Deer raised an eyebrow. 'Mr Merriweather, when you talk like that I never know whether you're being serious.'

Jacob smiled. 'That's because I've been trained as a lawyer, my friend. A lawyer learns to speak with a forked tongue. That's how he gets rich. But I can promise you one thing – I couldn't be more serious about those killers. I promised to bring them to justice, and I intend to carry out that promise even if it's the last thing I do . . . and you can carve that on my tombstone when I'm gone.'

Running Deer smiled. 'Well then, Mr Merriweather, I think we should talk to the others and lay out our plans. But first off I'm gonna tie Olsen to a tree well out of hearing so he doesn't get wind of what we aim to do.'

The four of them sat down by the fire for a council of war. Running Deer loaded his pipe with sweet grass tobacco and smoked with a reflective smile on his dark countenance. Old Sam sat on a large log; Marie sat cross-legged on the grass. And Jacob took a few steps towards the ruin and then stepped back.

'Well, folks, I need to make one thing clear,' he said, 'and that is, I aim to bring those killers to justice by fair means or foul.'

'What do you mean by foul?' Sam piped up.

Jacob squatted on his haunches, which brought him on a level with the others. 'What do I mean by foul?' he repeated. 'Well, I guess that means alive is better than dead, but it might mean dead if it comes to shooting, because it might be a matter of shoot or be shot. That's the grim reality, and before we go ahead I want you to understand that.'

Sam ran his fingers through his white beard. 'How can you bring a dead man to justice? If we kill Jack Davidson we might find ourselves on the wrong side of the law ourselves.'

'That's a point to consider,' Running Deer put in.

'True,' Jacob conceded. 'But consider this as well: we know that Stringer was one of the killers, but we don't know how many of Davidson's bunch are ready to kill for Davidson, do we?'

Sam held up his hand. 'As you know, I'm a man of peace, and I've never fired a shot in my life, and I don't mean to start now I'm in limping distance from the grave.'

'So you have a plan of your own?' Running Deer suggested.

'Well, yes I do,' the old man smiled. 'My plan is to ride up to the ranch-house door and tell Jack Davidson he's under arrest.'

They turned to him in amazement.

'You mean you'll ride right up to Davidson's door and tell him he's under arrest?' Jacob repeated.

Sam smiled. 'Well, that's what you aim to do, isn't it? Except that you'll have guns in your hands.'

Running Deer was on the point of laughing, but he held himself in out of respect for the old man.

Jacob took a deep breath and looked at Marie who had gone unexpectedly quiet. 'Now Sam, we all know you're a man of peace. So why don't you just escort Miss Marie back to town and let Running Deer and me do the arresting?'

'Except there's no way I'm going back to town without you,' Marie said.

'OK,' Jacob nodded. 'In that case we go on together, and' – he reached down and took a gun from his belt – 'you'd better take this for your protection. That Springfield of yours might be good enough in its way, but a six-shot pistol might be a lot better in a tight corner.' He held the gun by the barrel and Marie took it and examined it and then tucked it into her belt. 'I did shoot a rabid dog with one of these one time,' she said.

'Well, you shot a rabid Wolf down by the creek as well,' Running Deer said, 'and that saved both you and Mr Critchley here. And that's no small thing, is it?'

They rode on towards the Davidson spread, led by Running Deer who had Olsen ahead of him on a rope. Olsen had become quite passive, as though he had resigned himself to his rôle as arresting sheriff. Jacob rode several yards behind with Marie on his left and Sam on his right, riding his burro.

'Why don't I do the arresting?' Marie asked Jacob.

Jacob turned to look at her. 'Because I can't let you to do that, Marie. We have too much future before us.'

'I don't think I'm the woman you think I am, Jacob,' she said quietly.

'I think you're twice the woman I think you are,' Jacob replied.

Running Deer knew the country well, and he led them up through a wooded area where they were less exposed and from where they could look down through the cotton-woods to a long, sprawling plain where they saw many cattle grazing. Then he drew the party to a halt.

'This is the Davidson range,' he said. 'It might look big but it was a lot bigger when I was young.'

Jacob got out his spy glass and studied the herd. 'I see two riders down there,' he said. 'How many hands does Davidson run?'

Running Deer shrugged. 'Sometimes no more than six or seven, and sometimes as many as ten, depending on the time of year.'

Jacob was still studying the waddies through his spy-glass: 'I don't see Stringer down there.'

'I guess you won't,' Running Deer said, 'but he can't be far away. Now the other three have gone missing Davidson must guess we're coming for him. Have you thought about that?'

'Yes, I've thought about it a lot,' Jacob said. 'Where is the ranch house?'

Running Deer pointed to the West. 'It's over there a piece. If you look down there to your right where those waddies are riding you'll see the trail that leads right up to it.'

As they rode on, a grim silence fell between them. They were like soldiers riding into a battle where nobody could foresee the end. When they reached the top of the rise, Running Deer raised his hand and the party drew to a halt among the cottonwoods. Running Deer pointed at the plain below. 'That's the ranch house.'

Jacob took out his spyglass and studied the panorama. He saw a clapboard building rising grey and majestic from the plain. It was large enough to be called a mansion. In front of it was a fence and an entrance gate with the horns of a longhorn steer over it and an inscription he could just about read: *Circle Bar Ranch*.

'Well, that sure is something!' he murmured.

'That's the castle we have to invest,' Sam said like a medieval knight addressing his squire.

Olsen swung round. 'You know what you're riding into?' he asked. 'You think Davidson is a fool. If he's in there he'll be watching and waiting. You might as well be riding into the jaws of hell itself.'

'Well, we might be riding into the jaws of the Lord of this World,' Old Sam piped up, 'but we have the sword of righteousness in our hands.'

Olsen gave a sneering laugh. 'You might as well have a fairy's wand for all the good it will do you!'

'Well, you're about to wave that wand, my friend,' Jacob said, 'so you might as well make yourself good and ready.'

Olsen gave a croaking laugh. 'You're a bunch of hick fools!' he said. 'You have no idea what's waiting for you down there!'

'Well, we're about to find out,' Jacob replied, 'so lead the way!'

They jigged their horses forwards and rode down the long and gentle slope towards the ranch.

Jacob held his Winchester across his saddle and Running Deer covered Olsen with his six-gun. Marie rode close to Jacob on his left, and Old Sam rode beside him on his right. Jacob heard Sam humming quietly to himself as though he hadn't a care in the world. I guess that's what some folk call faith, he thought.

Jacob turned towards Marie. 'If there's any shooting, I want you to take care and keep out of trouble as much as you can. And if you have to use that shooter make sure you aim straight, because this is going to be a matter of kill or be killed.'

As they approached the gate with steer's horns above it, he was looking at the ranch house and he thought he saw the merest flutter of a curtain at an upstairs window. He half expected to hear a shot as they rode through the entrance gate, but all was menacingly quiet.

'This is my call,' Old Sam declared with quiet determination. He rode forwards, and then dismounted and walked up to the grand façade. There was a giant iron knocker in the shape of a steer's head on the door, and Sam seized it firmly and brought it down heavily three times. They heard the dull thud echoing through the ranch house.

Nobody spoke and nobody challenged the old man. He had asserted his right as an elder and they all waited in respect.

After what seemed like a century Jacob heard footsteps approaching, and he braced himself for whatever was to come. Then the door opened slowly and a dark female face peered out at them.

'Open up, my dear,' Sam said quietly. 'You have nothing to fear.'

The door opened wider to reveal a woman dressed in black clothes with white cuffs and a white lace collar. Her eyes were wide with surprise and fear. 'Can I help you?' she stammered.

'Is the master in?' Sam asked in a gentle tone.

The woman rolled her eyes and made no reply.

'What's your name, my dear?' Sam asked her.

Her lip trembled. 'My name's Mabel,' she said nervously.

'Well, now, Mabel, can you tell us where your master is?' Sam asked her.

She looked past Sam at the others and her eyes seemed to flutter with doubt. 'Master's from home,' she said. She was looking directly at Olsen. Olsen said nothing, but Jacob could see by the slight movement of his body that he was trying to convey a message of some kind.

'Well, now, Mabel,' Jacob said, 'when you see Mr Davidson. will you give him a message from us?'

'Yes, sir, I will.' Her lips were trembling even more. In fact her whole face seemed to be in motion.

'Tell Mr Davidson that Sheriff Olsen has called with an important message, will you?'

'Yes sir, I will. I'll tell him Mr Olsen called.' Her eyes darted towards Olsen and then looked away

'Are you sure there's nobody else in the house?' Sam asked her.

'Why, sure I'm sure, Master. Mr Jack is out on the ranch some place. Could be a mile or more away for all I know.'

Sam nodded and smiled. 'Well, be sure to give him the message when he comes home, will you, my dear?'

'I sure will, Master.' She pushed the door to and took one final look at them before closing it.

Jacob was looking all round suspiciously, but all he

could see were several very fine horses in the corral close to the house.

'What do you think?' Marie asked.

'I think the girl's lying,' Jacob said.

'Of course she's lying,' Old Sam interjected. 'And I don't blame her either. That poor girl is scared to death.'

'You're just a bunch of hick idiots,' Olsen burst out. 'Did you expect Davidson to just come to the door and say, "Here I am, gentlemen. I'm ready to give myself up and ride into town to face trial for murder"? D'you think the man's plumb crazy enough for that?'

Jacob laughed. 'Well, Sheriff, it seems you know him better than anyone else in this outfit. So maybe you can answer that question yourself.'

Olsen gave a snort. 'My guess is you'll all be stiff and dead before sunset.'

'In that case, what do you guess might happen to you?' Running Deer asked him.

Olsen shrugged and made no reply.

'The question is, what do we do now?' Running Deer said. 'Do we give up and ride back to town, or do we go down and ask those waddies if they've seen the boss?'

'Well, that's a fine laugh!' Olsen crowed. 'D'you think those boys are gonna spill the beans on anything at all? You might as well talk to your horse's arse!'

They were riding towards the gate with the steer's horns. Jacob thought, if Davidson wants us dead all he has to do is lean out of the upstairs window and spray us with a shotgun or shoot us one by one with a buffalo gun. But I don't think he'll be stupid enough for that. Nevertheless he looked over his shoulder and saw a top-floor window was open, and as he looked, he saw the faint flutter of a white kerchief. It wouldn't be Jack Davidson, but it could be the young servant girl giving some kind of signal . . . but to whom?

They were now approaching the gate, which meant they had to bunch together more closely, and that's when it happened. There was a sharp crack from the cotton woods.

'It seems we're under fire,' Sam said with surprising composure.

Jacob measured the distance with his eye. It was impossible to judge exactly where the shot had come from, but it had fallen well short of them. 'Out of range,' he said. 'They couldn't hit us from that distance. It was a warning shot.'

'What do you figure from that?' Running Deer asked him.

'I figure whoever fired that shot wanted us out of here,' Jacob said.

'So what do we do?'

'Well,' Jacob said, 'I didn't come all this way just to turn around and ride back again empty-handed. If I go back, Jack Davidson's coming with me.' He levelled his spyglass on the cottonwoods and thought he saw a movement among the trees. It was so faint he couldn't be sure that his eyes weren't deceiving him. 'I guess I'm going up there to investigate,' he said.

'You can't do that,' Marie protested. 'They'll be watching you all the way and they'll shoot you.'

'Not if I shoot them first,' Jacob said.

Running Deer was looking up at the belt of cotton-woods. 'If you're going up there, I'm coming right with you. Two guns are better than one.'

'Then I'm coming too,' Marie said.

Jacob swung round in the saddle. 'Please don't think of

it, Marie. You've done more than your share of gunsling-ing. Stay right here with Sam. If you come with us that'll be one more target for whoever's up there.'

Marie looked at him defiantly. 'Down here could be just as dangerous as up there. We don't know how many there are, do we?'

Then suddenly Olsen came to life. 'You want my opinion, that's Stringer up there and he's as deadly as a whole nest of rattlesnakes.'

'That's why you need to arrest him, Sheriff, and that's why you're coming up there with us.'

Olsen curled his lip in contempt, 'You can't arrest a man like Stringer without a gun, and I'm unarmed. In any case, he won't be waiting for you. By now he'll have got on his horse and ridden away to hell and back.'

'Well, wherever he's going I'm following him,' Jacob said. He turned to Marie again. 'Stick with Sam and hold that gun of yours ready.'

Jacob and Running Deer rode directly for the cotton-woods until they were within range of whatever Stringer could throw at them. Jacob held Olsen at rope's length in front of him. If anyone took a shot at him Olsen would also be in the firing line. Jacob had untied the sheriff's hands so he wasn't just a sitting duck.

Running Deer said, 'Two moving targets are better than one. So I'm riding off to the right here – and when we meet at the top of the bluff, don't shoot me by mistake.' He laughed and rode off at an angle towards the cotton-woods.

'OK,' Olsen said over his shoulder, 'I'm ready to do whatever's necessary. I don't like Stringer any more than you do, and he should swing for what he did to those two innocent people.'

'Why this sudden change of heart?' Jacob was about to ask him – but there was a sudden shot from above and Olsen jerked back. His horse reared and galloped away with Olsen still in the saddle.

Jacob had no time to wonder whether Olsen was dead or alive: he just brought his Peacemaker into line and fired. He knew he had little chance of hitting anyone, but at least it might deflect the gunman's aim. He took a quick look in Running Deer's direction and saw that he had already disappeared among the cottonwoods.

Jacob rode on recklessly and entered the woods right where he thought Stringer must have been, but there was no sign of him. He dismounted and knelt to read the signs. He found two spent cartridge cases on the ground. He looked up as Running Deer approached between the trees.

'You were lucky,' Running Deer told him. 'That shot was meant for you.'

'Did you see what happened to Olsen?' Jacob asked him.

'Last time I saw him he was riding hell for leather down to your right. He was certainly hit. He might be dead in the saddle or just wounded. So what do we do?'

'Like I said, there's no going back. So we ride after Stringer and bring him in. I'm a lucky son of a gun because you're a whole lot better as a tracker than I shall ever be.'

Running Deer stooped and examined the tracks. 'Well, it's not too difficult, Mr Merriweather. Lookee here. This is where Stringer ran back to his horse and this is where it was tethered. Then he mounted up and rode away as fast as he could. He shouldn't be too far ahead. So follow me.' He mounted his horse. 'But take care because with a customer like Stringer anything could happen.'

They rode on between the trees, which became denser. Stringer's tracks skirted round the dense part and made for the lower ground.

'He's headed for the lower ground and my guess he's leading us into a killing field. Stringer knows this country like the back of his hand. So he knows the best place to trap us and shoot us down. So watch yourself, Mr Merriweather, because this is gonna be some picnic.' A few paces later he held up his hand and they stopped. They had reached the edge of the wood. Running Deer dismounted and surveyed the terrain ahead. 'Lookee there.' He pointed through the trees. 'Luckily I know this country as well. Probably a lot better. If we ride down there we might just as well ask to be fried because we'll be riding right where he wants us to be.'

Jacob was scanning the country below through his spyglass. The land fell away in a series of humps to the plain below. He moved his spyglass to the right where there were several commanding heights that looked down on to the flat country. He saw no sign of Stringer or anyone else.

'Give me that glass,' Running Deer said. Jacob handed over the spyglass and Running Deer looked towards the commanding heights. 'Yes, yes,' he muttered to himself. 'That's where they'll be.'

'You mean Stringer isn't alone?' Jacob asked him.

Running Deer shook his head. 'My guess is there could be others, maybe a whole bunch of them.' He handed back the spyglass and Jacob focused it on the commanding position where Stringer would be concealed. 'So, we could be in deep shit here,' he speculated.

'Well, if we ride down there we'll be in Stringer's sights all the way, but we're not gonna do that, Mr Merriweather.

I know a better way.' Running Deer pointed way to the right where the bluff rose even higher. 'We go that way. If we keep to the high ground we can come out above them.'

'Can we do that?' Jacob asked him.

Running Deer nodded and grinned. 'Follow me, Mr Merriweather, and don't hurry. We don't want to show our hand until we have to.' He turned his horse back into the cottonwoods and rode cautiously on.

Jacob followed him closely as they climbed to the high country.

CHAPTER NINE

Jacob was glad Running Deer was leading the way. This land was in the marrow of his bones and Jacob couldn't help wondering how he had become so deeply embedded in so-called civilized culture. From the way Running Deer let his horse amble along you would have thought he was simply taking the air on a quiet Sunday afternoon, except that he paused occasionally to raise his head and sniff the air as though whatever lay ahead might be wafted on the air towards them.

Then he stopped and motioned to Jacob. Jacob drew up beside him and Running Deer spoke to him as quietly as the wind rustling the leaves in the trees.

'Now we leave the forest and ride up to the right of this bluff ahead. It might seem a long way off our track, but it leads us behind and above where Stringer will be. But we'll wait here a piece so the horses can take a bite of grass and get their wind.' He dismounted and clamped his pipe between his teeth. But he didn't light up. 'The wind is coming from over the top of the hill, but we won't take any chances.'

The two men squatted down and rested briefly while the horses grazed in the long grass at the edge of the forest.

Jacob thought of Marie and Sam Critchley back at the ranch house, and wondered how they were faring. Running Deer looked at him and nodded as though he read his thoughts.

'That woman has a lot of grit,' he said. 'I've known her quite some time but I've never seen before quite how strong she is.' He smiled. 'Meeting you has made all the difference, Mr Merriweather. It's kind of brought her out, if you understand me.'

'Well, Running Deer, it's kind of brought me out, too. And by the way, don't keep calling me Mr Merriweather. Makes me feel sort of superior.'

'OK, Jake.' Running Deer held out his hand and they shook. 'I guess we'd better ride on and get this thing all rolled up and sorted out.'

They mounted up and rode on. Now they were clear of the cottonwoods Running Deer rode more cautiously, watching for signs all the way. They rode to the high ground, keeping the bluff on their left. It seemed a long way to Jacob, but Running Deer knew his business and Jacob was glad to follow. Once Running Deer held up his hand and listened, and they heard the distant whinnying of a horse.

As they drew close to the top of the bluff, Running Deer held up his hand again and paused, and Jacob drew in beside him. 'Tell you something, Jake. We're not alone, so keep your gun handy.'

Jacob drew his Peacemaker and held it steady. Suddenly a figure appeared before them. It wasn't Stringer or Jack Davidson: it was a man Jacob had never seen before. He was tall in the saddle and he was dressed in range clothes – and he held a six-shot Remington in his hand.

'Well, now,' the man said, 'look what we have here.'

119

There was a note of sarcasm in his voice and he was smiling, but it was none too friendly a smile.

Jacob drew alongside Running Deer. Running Deer's advice had been timely. So Jacob held his Peacemaker level.

'You just out for a ride, or have you something particular in mind?' the man asked in the same sarcastic tone.

Running Deer nodded. 'What's particular?' he asked.

The man grinned. 'Particular is the fact you're on private land. Maybe you didn't know that.'

Jacob tightened his grip on his gun. 'As a matter of fact, we have an appointment with Mr Davidson, but it seems he isn't at home right now.'

The man looked at Jacob and nodded. 'And who would you be? You look like a lawyer and you talk like a lawyer, but I see you're carrying a shooter.'

Jacob smiled but kept his eyes firmly on the other man. In his experience you could always tell by a man's eyes when he was about to draw.

'Well, sir, I carry a gun because I've met a lot of strange customers since I came out West and you're never sure how a man will react, are you?'

'That is so,' the man agreed. 'And that's why I'm here, too.'

Jacob pointed his Peacemaker directly at the waddy. 'In which case,' he said, 'maybe you'll be kind enough to drop that Remington in case I have to shoot you.'

The man's eyes widened, and for a moment he hesitated. He looked straight into the barrel of Jacob's gun and Jacob gave a slight gesture to indicate that indeed he might shoot him. Then the man lowered his gun and let it drop. 'What do you want with me, sir?' he asked.

'Well, first of all you can dismount and answer a few questions.'

The man hesitated for moment, then dismounted and made to retrieve his gun.

'Don't even think about it,' Jacob said.

Jacob looked at Running Deer, and Running Deer dismounted and picked up the man's gun and stuck it through his belt.

'What are the questions?' the man asked.

Jacob paused. 'Now I want you to understand this,' he said. 'If you play this off the top of the pack you might live another day or two. If you fool around with us you most likely will not. Do I make myself clear?'

'You make yourself good and clear,' the man said evenly.

'Well now,' Jacob said, 'the questions are, first, why are you up here on the bluff standing in our way? And where are Stringer and Jack Davidson?'

The man went slightly pale under his tan. 'I can't answer that.'

'Well now,' Jacob said. 'Let me take a guess. You're a simple cowpoke, but you have ambitions. Would that be true?'

The man grinned. 'Well, yes, sir, I do have ambitions.'

Jacob nodded. 'A man doesn't want to spend the rest of his life riding herd, does he?'

The cowpoke grinned at him. 'I don't want a difference of opinion with you, sir. Leastways not while you've got a gun pointed directly at me. The answer to your question is I don't know where the boss is. He could be anywhere between here and Amarillo.'

Jacob nodded, 'But you do know where Stringer is?'

The man looked somewhat doubtful. 'Stringer isn't a man to be crossed. He's quick with a gun and he's got a bite like a rattlesnake.'

Jacob nodded. 'I guess that's so.' He smiled at the man. 'Did you happen to come across Wolf and a man called Killop in your travels?'

The man's eyes narrowed. 'Sure. They were part of the Davidson outfit.'

'Well, you might be interested to know that Wolf is lying dead by a creek somewhere between here and town and he's not a pretty sight, what with the coyotes and the buzzards chewing away at his body. And Killop is languishing in jail waiting to testify against Stringer and Jack Davidson for murder.'

The man turned a shade paler. 'I don't know anything about that,' he said.

Jacob was grinning. 'So maybe you'd be kind enough to tell us where Stringer is right now?'

The man looked to his right where they had guessed Stringer would be. 'He's down there waiting for you.'

Running Deer spoke up. 'Is he alone?'

The man shook his head. 'There's a couple of the boys with him. But they're just obeying orders. They don't know what this is about.'

'Well, I guess they don't read the news-sheets.' Jacob told him in some detail about the murder of the two inno-cents. 'So we've come to arrest Stringer and take him back to town on trial for murder.'

A look of amazement appeared on the waddy's face. 'I didn't know a thing about that.'

'Well, now you do. The question is, will you help us, or won't you?' Jacob asked him.

The waddy shook his head. 'How do I know you're on the level?'

'Well, I can't show you my badge of office. Sheriff Olsen got shot back there and he took his badge with him. He's probably been killed, but we don't know yet. Maybe you were with Stringer when the shot was fired. You might even have fired it yourself.'

'Well, I didn't fire the shot because I wasn't there,' the man said.

Jacob glanced at Running Deer and Running Deer's expression said, 'This man's lying through his teeth.'

'OK,' Jacob said. 'Now you're going to lead the way down to where Stringer's hiding out waiting to gun down on us, and if you make a good job of it, you might live to fight another day. If not, who knows? You hear me?'

'I hear you loud and clear,' the man said.

They mounted up and rode down to where they figured Stringer was waiting. It was impossible to conceal themselves since there was scarcely any ground cover, just scree and rocks and the occasional stunted shrub.

'What do you expect me to do?' the waddy asked Jacob.

'Just keep going till I say stop,' Jacob told him.

They started riding down the incline. Then they heard a voice from below. 'Is that you, Bowdene?'

'That's Stringer,' Bowdene said. 'What do I say to him?'

'Just tell him we're coming to get him,' Jacob said.

Bowdene opened his mouth to speak but no words came out. It was too late, anyway. Suddenly from below Stringer appeared and he was fan palming his gun. Bullets flew in quick succession all round the approaching group.

Jacob flung himself from his horse and the other two followed.

'My gawd!' Bowdene exclaimed, 'He's set to kill us all.'

Stringer suddenly stopped firing. Fan palming uses a lot of ammunition but you're lucky if you hit anyone. Stringer was now either drawing another gun or pausing to reload.

Jacob sprang up from the ground and ran forward until

he was just a few yards from where Stringer was crouching. As he ran he saw two men scrambling down the scree away from the action. He stopped and levelled his gun, but before he could bring it to bear, Stringer raised his weapon and hurled it straight at Jacob's face. It struck Jacob on the jaw and he fell back, firing the Peacemaker into the air. The bullet went wide and Jacob lay prostrate, shaking his head and trying to roll away. Through the mist in his head Jacob heard an insistent voice telling him if he didn't move fast he'd be a dead man.

When he opened his eyes again, he saw a face peering down at him. For a moment he wondered who it could be, but then his eyes came into focus and he recognized Bowdene. What the hell's happening here? he thought.

'Lie still,' Bowdene said. 'Wait till you get yourself together, man.'

Jacob sat up and worked his jaw. It felt as though it had been hit by a locomotive in full steam.

'Take it easy,' Bowdene said. 'At least you're alive, man.'

Jacob heard shots. 'Who's shooting?' he tried to ask but his voice came out in a muffled croak.

'It's that Injun friend of yours. He's shooting at Stringer.'

Jacob swung round and looked below and saw Running Deer kneeling close by and firing at several retreating figures below. 'What the hell's going on here?' he managed to croak out.

Bowdene gave a low growl of mirth. 'My buddies are making a tactical retreat,' he said. 'And Stringer is running for his horse. Pity your friend is such a bad shot.'

Jacob squinted at him. 'How come you've suddenly become so damned friendly?'

Bowdene shrugged. 'You told me I should play my cards

124

off the top of the pack, and that was good advice. And, by the way, here's your gun, and don't worry, I won't shoot you. But after Stringer tried to kill us all I figured it was time to act in the cause of righteousness.'

Jacob took his gun and cocked it, but he didn't fire. Stringer was already on his horse, picking his way among the rocks to the plain below, and the other two were well ahead on their horses.

'Don't waste your bullets,' Bowdene advised. 'Stringer has a damned fine horse and he'll be down in the flat country before you can say "gig up, boy".'

Running Deer was running back for his horse. He paused and looked at Jacob, who was somewhat unsteady on his feet. 'You look like you've been hit by a rock.'

Bowdene bent down and picked up Stringer's gun. 'Don't worry,' he said. 'Like I thought it isn't loaded. D'you figure you're jaw's out of joint?'

Jacob worked his jaw and winced. 'I guess it will do for now.'

'Well, my friend,' Bowdene, said 'you look like you've been hit by the heavyweight champion of the world. The ladies won't find you too attractive 'til it heals. Tell you the truth, you look like Big Foot, though I haven't seen that ugly beast myself.'

Running Deer didn't look amused. 'You want me to tie up your face with a bandanna, help you heal ?'

Jacob shook his head a little. 'Just bring my horse and I'll mount up. We've got to catch up on Stringer before he does any more damage to the world.'

Bowdene gave a sceptical grin. 'There's no way we're gonna catch up on Stringer. He could be half way to Texas by now.'

'That's what I'm afraid off,' Jacob said. He mounted up,

and the other two did likewise.

'Well, that *hombre* sure has grit,' Bowdene said to Running Deer.

'You better believe it,' Running Deer replied.

Bowdene chuckled.

Jacob rode down through the high country towards the plain. He could still see the three riders well ahead below him, but he realized he had no chance of catching them up. He felt like hell, but as soon as he got into the saddle his head began to clear. He reined in and turned to Running Deer. 'I figure Bowdene's right. We're riding in the wrong direction. Stringer can wait. However deadly he might be, we have to catch the big fish.'

'So what do you aim to do?' Running Deer asked.

'I'm going to turn my horse and head straight back to the ranch. I guess I've been stupid. I need to know what's happening to Marie and Old Sam.'

'Well, that sounds like good thinking to me,' Running Deer agreed.

As they were turning their horses, Bowdene stopped and asked, 'Where do I fit in here?'

Running Deer and Jacob exchanged glances. 'Well, Mr Bowdene,' Jacob said, 'you don't fit in anywhere. So what I suggest is this: you turn your horse and ride anywhere you want and do your best to fulfil those ambitions sprouting in your head, and water them good to make them grow strong. But don't come back in case I have to shoot you.'

Bowdene grinned and nodded. 'Well, thanks for that. I appreciate it.'

Merriweather turned to Running Deer. 'Why don't you give the man his gun, my friend?'

Running Deer took the Remington from his belt and shucked out the shells and handed it over to Bowdene.

Still grinning, Bowdene took the Remingon and slid it into its holster and said, '*Adios, amigos.* Nice doing business with you.' Then he turned and rode away to the west.

'You figure we can trust him?' Running Deer said.

Jacob nodded. 'Trust every man,' he said, 'but keep your back to the wall in case he takes a pop at you. I can think of two well-known gunslingers who didn't live to learn that important lesson. That's why I'm going to keep my eyes at the back of my head as we ride back to the ranch house to confront that big rancher Jack Davidson.'

They rode through the cottonwoods towards the ranch house without seeing a single soul.

'I just hope our two friends are OK,' Running Deer said.

They emerged from the belt of cottonwoods. The ranch house looked surprisingly tranquil with Davidson's thoroughbred horses chewing contentedly in the corral and grey smoke spiralling up from the chimney as though time would last for ever and a day. But there was no sign of Old Sam or Marie or their mounts.

'What to we do now?' Running Deer asked.

'Only one thing to do: we ride down and inquire,' Jacob said.

They rode under the arch with the steer horns and on towards the house. As they drew close, the door opened and a man appeared. He was dressed in a fine suit of well spun wool and his thumbs were hooked into a fancy vest rather like Jacob's namesake's coat of many colours. Though he had little hair on his head and was somewhat portly, he looked like a rather over-pampered forty-year-old schoolboy with a superior glint in his eye.

'That's Jack Davidson,' Running Deer muttered quietly.

Jacob steadied himself in the saddle. 'Good day to you, sir,' he greeted in as plummy a voice as he could manage. 'I wonder if you can tell me whether you've seen our two friends?'

Davidson gave a charming but artificial smile, rather like the fixed grin on the face of a gargoyle. 'Well, good sir, I haven't seen anyone in the last hour, but my maid did mention there were four callers earlier, or maybe it was five, but since I rode back I haven't seen a single soul. So sorry to disappoint you, gentlemen.'

With that he turned away and was about to close the door when he had a sudden change of mind and turned back. 'You must have ridden a long way, gentlemen. Perhaps you'd care to come in and take some refreshment?' He looked directly at Jacob. 'If you don't mind me saying so, good sir, your face looks in real bad shape, like you've been hit by a locomotive.'

Jacob did his best to smile. 'Well, good sir. I do believe we will accept your generous offer.'

Davidson gave a stiff bow. 'Then please step inside and I'll have one of my men corral your horses so they can rest up. They do look a little tuckered out.' He gave a somewhat sinister chuckle and stepped aside to admit them.

Jacob looked at Running Deer and gave him an encouraging nod. Running Deer raised an eyebrow and followed him in.

They found themselves in a large room, which reminded Jacob of a fancy palace in a vulgar fairy tale. There were large glass chandeliers suspended from the ceiling, and a welcoming fire burning on the hearth, which was a luxury on such a warm day.

Davidson gestured towards the fire. 'Please be seated, gentlemen. I would have been happy to invite you to dinner, but it's a little too early. So we'll have to be content with some of our home brew and a few biscuits baked on the premises.'

'Well, thank you, sir,' Jacob looked at Running Deer and they both sat down in soft seats beside the fire. Running Deer looked a little like a fish stranded in an unfamiliar pool.

Davidson rang a bell and a man in livery entered by a distant door, holding a tray laden with biscuits and fancy glasses, and a bottle of liquor that didn't look like home brew at all!

Jacob glanced at the servant and thought he looked more like a domesticated thug than a servant, and he had a suspicious-looking bulge under his jacket. The servant gave him a quick glance, but it wasn't quite quick enough. Jacob had drawn his gun and pointed it directly at Jack Davidson. 'Well, now, Mr Davidson, I think it's time to get down to business. If you'll be kind enough to ask your servant to hold up his hands, my friend here will relieve him of that gun he has concealed in his shoulder holster. Otherwise somebody's likely to have a serious accident.'

Davidson scarcely batted an eyelid. Then he nodded at the servant. 'Do as the gentleman says, Arnold.'

Arnold raised his hands and Running Deer reached under his arm and relieved him of his Smith & Wesson revolver.

Davidson was still grinning. 'Is this highway robbery?' he asked.

'No,' Jacob replied. 'It's just part of the business in hand.'

Davidson was still holding his glass. 'Then may I

enquire about the nature of your business?'

Jacob stood up from the table but kept his Peacemaker levelled on Jack Davidson. 'The business in hand is I'm arresting you for the murder of two innocent young people by the name of Beth and Stan Salinger on a small-holding between here and town a few weeks back.'

Daivdson's jaw tightened, but he continued to grin. 'Well, I read about that in the news-sheet but I think you've got the wrong idea. I never killed a man or woman in my life.'

'You didn't need to,' Running Deer interjected. 'You hired four gunmen to do your dirty work for you.'

'Well, that's an interesting theory,' Davidson said, 'but who might these gunmen be, assuming they exist?'

Jacob chuckled. 'Well, they did exist, Mr Davidson, but one of them by the name of Wolf is being eaten by the coyotes right now, and a big guy I never caught the name of is lying in the funeral parlour back in town waiting to be put into the ground.'

Davidson nodded. 'I'm sure sorry to hear about that. Those two rowdy characters did work for me for a time, but I had to let them go. Pity they got themselves killed.'

'What about Stringer?' Jacob asked him.

'What about Stringer?' Davidson actually turned a little paler under his tan.

'Well, if you'd been listening hard an hour or so back you might have heard the sound of gunfire. That was when your man Stringer took a pop at us. Unfortunately, he hit the wrong man in the shape of Sheriff Olsen.'

'Olsen!' Davidson said in some surprise.

'That's right – Olsen,' Jacob repeated. 'Indeed, he would be here to arrest you himself, but unfortunately his horse bolted and we don't know whether he's dead or alive.'

Davidson's eyes slid towards his manservant, but for a moment he said nothing. Jacob could see his mind ticking over somewhat faster, but Davidson continued to grin. Then he spoke again. 'This is a whole pack of lies you're telling me!' he snarled. 'What right have you to come into a gentleman's home and threaten him and make such preposterous allegations?'

Jacob shrugged. 'Well, they may be preposterous, sir, and you'll have a chance to prove that in court. So I hope you have a good lawyer.'

'Well, I sure do!' Davidson declared. 'And I tell you this. If this ever comes to court, you'll be the ones in jail, not me.'

'Well,' Jacob said, 'now we've got that sorted out, there are only two things to do.'

'And what might they be?' Davidson asked defiantly.

Jacob turned to the manservant. 'Arnold, my good man, I want you to accompany my friend Running Deer here and take him to where Sam Critchley and a young lady called Marie are being held. Then you can tell one of your stable hands to release them and bring out our horses and saddle up one of those fine thoroughbreds, so Mr Davidson can ride back to town with the dignity that becomes a gentleman. And by the way, I'm sure Mr Davidson would hate to lose a good servant, even if he is to be away for quite a stretch. So keep the house in order while he's away.'

CHAPTER TEN

Arnold the manservant was like a good old English butler, apart from the fact he had had a gun in a shoulder holster. He remained calm and his face expressed no emotion as he carried out his orders, but as Jacob observed, his eyes told a different story. 'Don't turn your back on that guy for a second,' he told himself.

When Marie and Old Sam were released from the lock-up they reacted very differently. Old Sam even thanked the stable hand and manservant. 'I knew you'd see reason soon enough,' he said to Davidson. 'It never pays to lock up innocent folk. It always comes back on you in the end.'

Davidson responded in kind. 'Well, my friend, sometimes a man has to be locked up for his own protection.'

'True, true,' Sam agreed. 'And that's why we have the law in this great land of ours.'

Marie wasn't so calm. In fact she looked pale with fury. 'And maybe you'll return my gun.' she said.

'Of course,' Davidson replied. 'Give the lady back her gun, Arnold. But take good care in case it goes off by mistake, which would be an awful pity, wouldn't it?'

Arnold gave a faint smirk as he handed the weapon back. Marie stuck it through her belt and mounted her horse.

Jacob turned to Davidson. 'Now, I warn you, Mr Davidson, we're going to ride back to town nice and easy and there aren't going to be any hitches, you hear me?'

Davidson's face twisted in a smug grin: 'You don't know what you're doing here,' he said. 'You might as well have put your hand in a pit full of snakes!'

'Well, I'll just have to take my chance on that, won't I?' Jacob replied.

When they were all mounted up, Davidson turned to the manservant and said, 'Now remember what I told you, Arnold.'

'Don't worry, Mr Davidson,' Arnold replied. Jacob wondered what the manservant was being told to remember, but he didn't press the point.

They rode off in a stately cavalcade with Davidson in the lead like a lord leading his retinue, and Jacob and Running Deer just behind him, and Marie and Old Sam on his burro in the rear.

It was some twenty miles to town, which shouldn't have taken much more than an hour and half, assuming there were no interruptions. And after twenty minutes there was a major interruption: from their right a horse came trotting towards them with a man leaning forwards in the saddle. At first Jacob thought it might be Stringer, but then he saw it was Sheriff Olsen. Olsen was leaning so far forward in the saddle he was set to fall. How he had managed to stay on his horse was beyond belief.

'Stay here,' Jacob said to Running Deer, 'and keep a weather eye on Davidson.'

He trotted over to Olsen and dismounted. 'So you're still alive!' he marvelled.

Olsen opened one eye and peered down at Jacob and Jacob saw he had a mess of blood on his chest. 'I thought maybe I could get back to town before I died,' he said in a hoarse whisper.

'Where are you hit?' Jacob asked him.

Olsen gritted his teeth and said, 'Up in the left shoulder. I guess it broke my collar bone. It hurts awful bad, I think I passed out but somehow I still kept on my horse.'

'You think you can dismount?' Jacob asked him.

Olsen grunted. 'If I get off this horse I shall never get back on again.'

Jacob mounted up. 'Let me take a look at that wound.' He leaned over Olsen and examined his shoulder. 'Well, there's good news and bad news,' he said.

'Just give me the good news,' Olsen croaked.

'The good news is I think the bullet passed right through.'

'The bad news is I think I might bleed to death,' Olsen said.

Jacob looked at the others and saw Running Deer riding towards him. 'Don't worry about Davidson,' Running Deer said. 'Marie knows how to use that gun if needs be.'

He drew close and examined Olsen's shoulder. 'Yeah, yeah,' he murmured, 'First thing we do is stop the bleeding.' He produced a spare shirt from somewhere and made it into a pad. 'Try to sit up a little and I'll strap it to your body to stop the bleeding.' He took Olsen by his good arm and helped him up a little. Olsen gritted his teeth to stop crying out. Running Deer then produced a small bottle of what looked like whiskey and poured some over the wound, and Olsen cried out in agony. 'It might hurt but it should keep the wound clean,' Running Deer told Olsen. Then he bound up the wound tight enough to staunch the flow of blood. 'Now, if you ride slow and steady you should survive long enough to see your wife back in town. Just hold on to the saddle horn and I'll lead you home.'

'Thank you, Running Deer,' the sheriff whispered hoarsely.

Running Deer took the horse's reins and they were ready to ride on.

Jacob drew alongside Marie. 'Well, whatever you might think of Olsen, you have to admire his grit. Not many *hombres* would have survived that shot. And he's our ace in the hole. So we have to ride real gently back to town and hope he will survive.'

'And that Stringer doesn't turn tail and try to finish the job,' Marie said.

'My guess is we've seen the last of Stringer. Guys like that are brave when they have a gun in their hand and they're shooting from cover, but out in the open they're not quite so gutsy. And Stringer won't be keen to swing for those murders either.'

'You mean he's going to get away with it?' Marie said.

Jacob held his head on one side. 'Sooner or later someone or something will catch up with him. Some might call it Fate. Others might call it justice. Whatever it is, it will happen in the long run.'

They rode on slowly but steadily towards town. Jack Davidson said nothing, though he had seen and heard everything.

It was getting towards sundown when at last they saw the yellow and orange gleam from the windows as they approached town.

'What do we do with Davidson?' Marie asked Jacob.

Jacob had been considering it all the way back to town.

135

But the problem was solved immediately when Davidson turned in the saddle and said, 'I aim to stay in the Grand hotel while I'm in town, which will only be for a few days, I promise you.'

When they reached the outskirts of town there was hardly a soul around. Folk were either in their houses or gathered in the saloons. As they rode in they could hear the tinkle of a honky-tonk piano and the scrape off fiddle strings. As usual there were a few loungers hanging around, and one of them looked up and said, 'Is that the sheriff I see?'

Olsen made no reply. He was still struggling to stay in the saddle and keep himself steady.

'Ride on to the sawbones,' Jacob said. 'We have to keep this man alive.'

They rode straight to the town doctor's house, which was somewhat grander than most of the other houses, and Jacob dismounted and rang the elaborately carved bell. After a minute or two the door was opened by the doctor himself. He looked straight at Olsen and gasped. 'Why, Sheriff, you've been wounded!'

Then suddenly Davidson spoke up. 'Shot by a man who used to work for me, a guy called Stringer who went to the bad. Olsen's taken a slug in the shoulder. Please do all you can to save him, at my expense, sir.'

The doctor looked up at Olsen and Olsen opened one eye. 'Please tell my wife I'm back,' he said faintly.

'The first thing is to get him off that horse without opening the wound,' the doc said.

Marie and Old Sam steadied the horse while Jacob and Running Deer, directed by the doctor, lifted Olsen down and carried him into the doctor's surgery and laid him on a bed. Olsen groaned as they carried him in, but as soon

136

as he was on the bed he closed his eyes and breathed deeply, and despite his pain, fell asleep.

Jacob and the rest of the party rode on to the Grand hotel. Davidson dismounted and handed the reins to Hank, the boy, who was waiting outside the hotel.

'Take this horse to the stable, boy, and make sure you look after him well because I'll be staying for a few days.' He stepped on to the sidewalk and turned in a somewhat masterful way. 'I hope you know what you've done here,' he said. 'You guys are dead in your boots, and you don't know it. So have a really good night's sleep because you're sure going to need it.'

They went to Running Deer's place, and Running Deer's wife Sophie greeted her husband as though he'd been to hell and back and managed to come through. Running Deer gave her an account of all that had happened. She listened attentively. 'You mean you've got Davidson in the lock-up?'

'No, he's staying in the Grand hotel.'

Sophie's eyes widened. 'You mean the man who killed Beth and Stan Salinger is staying in the best hotel in town?'

'Well, money can buy almost anything,' Jacob said, 'but he won't be there for more than a day or two since the long arm of the law is reaching out to grab him. But right now we have to go over and give Mrs Olsen the good news that her husband's still in the land of the living.'

But Mrs Olsen wasn't at home: she was right beside her husband's bed holding his good hand. The doctor had given the sheriff a sleeping draught so he was well away in the land of dreams. Marie sat beside her and attempted to comfort her. Outside the room Jacob spoke to the doc.

'You think he'll live?'

The doctor who had learned to be a profound pessimist held his head on one side. 'Well, this man is strong but he's lost a lot of blood. After a good night's rest and a bowl of my wife's rich soup, he could pull through. So why don't you look in in the morning?'

Jacob waited for Marie. Despite the hour, quite a crowd had gathered outside the surgery demanding to know what was happening. Among them was an eager young guy with a pad and pencil in hand. He was the local news-sheet owner. 'Can you tell me what's happening, sir?'

Jacob said, 'There isn't much to say. Sheriff Olsen's been shot, but we hope he will survive.'

'Has this got something to do with the Salinger killings, sir?'

Jacob smiled and shook his head. 'I'm afraid we can't comment on that for the moment.'

The news-sheet owner was scribbling vigorously on his pad.

Jacob and Marie walked across Main Street towards Marie's cabin.

'Tell me, Jacob, what are your intentions towards me?' she asked.

Jacob smiled. 'Nothing but honourable, I can assure you.'

Marie smiled back. 'Then maybe you'll be kind enough to step into the witch's den and share a brew. I guess you must be tired after all that's happened.'

Jacob took off his Stetson and bowed, 'I'd be glad to, ma'am. But first I have a small visit to make.'

'And what would that be, sir?'

'I think I'd better look in on the town jail and make sure a certain prisoner by the name of Killop is safe and sound.'

On the way to the jail he met Running Deer and another man: 'This here is Steve Tyler,' Running Deer introduced, 'Steve is Sheriff Olsen's deputy.'

Tyler stretched out his hand. 'I'm right pleased to meet you, sir. Glad to report the prisoner is good and safe, and we've been feeding him up good at the town's expense while you've been away. How's the sheriff? I hear he's been shot.'

'Shot in the shoulder,' Running Deer said. 'There's a good chance he'll pull through.'

'That's good to hear,' Tyler said. 'He's a good man, and a right good friend. He didn't deserve to be shot.'

'Well, I hope Killop isn't sleeping right now,' Jacob said, 'because I aim to look in and give him the gladsome tidings.'

Killop was sitting on his cot looking none too pleased. 'What's happening?' he asked when he saw Jacob. 'I heard the sheriff's been shot.'

'I'm afraid you heard right,' Jacob said. 'And Jack Davidson is holed up in the Grand hotel, at his own expense.'

Killop looked somewhat uneasy, 'Given the chance, Davidson will have me killed.'

Jacob nodded sagaciously. 'He'll be a damned fool if he does. Right now he'll be figuring out how he can hire the best lawyer in the county. Tomorrow morning early I'll be over to talk to you. So I hope you'll be good and ready.'

Running Deer gave Jacob a sly smile. 'I guess I know where you'll be staying the night, my friend.'

'And I guess you could be right, ' Jacob said.

'Well, don't wear yourself out,' Running Deer said, 'because you're gonna be awful busy tomorrow. Old Sam has gone to pick up his beloved wagon. I guess he'll be sleeping there tonight, dreaming of the heavenly spheres.'

When Jacob stepped into Marie's cabin, he saw she had changed out of her range clothes into a more feminine outfit, and there was a hint of sweet perfume wafting in the air. Jacob had been exhausted, but he soon felt the blood beginning to pulse through his veins.

'Sit down and eat,' Marie invited.

'I don't think so,' Jacob said. He took Marie into his arms and they kissed, and their kiss lasted so long they forgot that the food might be getting cold.

'If you're a witch then I'm a wizard,' he whispered when they broke away.

'In that case we'll climb on to our magic carpet and ride away together,' she murmured.

They woke to the sound of cock crow. 'Are you ready for breakfast?' Marie asked him.

'I could eat a whole herd of buffalo with a few deer thrown in,' he said.

'Well, you'll have to be content with eggs and ham. Sophie's just brought over a whole chunk of ham. She has an ice box where she keeps all kinds of food.'

They sat across the table from one another and ate.

'So how do we figure out the day?' she asked him.

Jacob looked thoughtful. 'Well, there are two things we need to take into account,' he said.

'And what would they be?'

'First, how we're going to bring Jack Davidson to justice.'

'And the second? '

They were both smiling.

'How and when we're going to make respectable folk of ourselves. And that's not the order of preference, by the way; that's the order of necessity.'

Jacob strapped on his gunbelt and walked down to the town jail where Killop was having his chow, watched over by Deputy Sheriff Jim Tyler.

'Good morning, Mr Merriweather,' the deputy greeted.

'Good morning, Mr Tyler. D'you mind if I have a few words with Mr Killop here?'

'Not at all, sir. I'll just step across and see how Sheriff Olsen is doing.'

Jacob sat down with Killop in his cell. 'Like I said, we need to have a talk,' Jacob said.

'I know that,' Killop acknowledged. Though he looked kind of wary, there was a gleam of determination in his eye.

Jacob paused for a moment. 'This is a big thing you're doing. When the time comes you must take the stand and tell the truth, the whole truth and nothing but the truth.'

'I know the truth,' Killop said, 'Jack Davidson paid four of us to kill those young people, but when it came to it I couldn't go through with it.'

'So you took the money and split?'

Killop frowned. 'That's the truth, Mr Merriweather. I'm not proud of taking the money, but I'm glad I had no part in killing those innocent kids.'

Jacob nodded. 'I guess you know all those killers have paid with their lives. That is, except Stringer who shot Sheriff Olsen. But my guess is Stringer has ridden off some place and we may never see him again.'

Killop grimaced. 'Stringer's as slippery as a jack fish, so I wouldn't count on that.'

Jacob nodded again. 'So are you ready to stand up in court and testify that you were there when your buddies shot down those innocent young people?'

Killop twisted his face in a frown. 'Just as long as it's clear that I didn't have any part in that killing.'

Jacob jotted down a note on his notepad. 'OK, Mr Killop. Enjoy your breakfast. I'll talk to you again later.'

Jacob walked across Main Street to the doctor's surgery.

'How's the patient?' he asked the doctor.

'Well, he's made of tough rawhide, so I think he'll survive for a while longer. His wife's with him right now, together with Deputy Tyler. They're having a good old confabulation about the future. But we don't want to tire him out, so maybe you should wait for a while.'

Jacob sat in the outer room twiddling his thumbs impatiently and watching the minutes tick inexorably by.

When he went into the sick room Sheriff Olsen was sitting up with his left arm bound up, but looking wide awake and eager.

'So,' he smiled, 'I guess I have to thank you for saving my life, Mr Merriweather.'

'Well, Running Deer did most of the saving, but I'm glad we got you home in time, no thanks to that guy Stringer who thought he had shot you dead. I guess you know your friend Jack Davidson is living it up in the Grand hotel right now?'

Olsen gave a mournful grin. 'I used to count Davidson among my friends, but I think I might need to strike him off my Christmas card list now.'

'That could be a wise decision,' Jacob agreed. 'I don't think the Devil appreciates Christmas cards that much, anyway. But whatever you think of Davidson, I guess you should prepare yourself for a visit.'

Olsen gave a faint nod. 'Jack Davidson is a tough and cunning *hombre*, Mr Merriweather, and I think you should be aware of that. But don't worry. I've asked Deputy Tyler to send a wire through to the county judge. He'll set things in motion for a trial. But I should warn you, Jack Davidson has a lot of friends and a great deal of influence, and he has enough money to hire the best lawyers. So you have a tough fight on your hands. And if you lose, you might be in the shit right up to your neck or maybe higher.'

Jacob walked over Main Street just as Old Sam emerged on the seat of his painted wagon. He drew his team to a halt and wagged his Santa Claus beard at Jacob. 'How's the sheriff?' he sang out.

'He's doing much better than anyone could have expected,' Jacob told him.

'Well, that's fine,' Old Sam said. 'The sooner we've buttoned this grisly business up, the better it will be for everyone concerned.'

Later that day a wire came through from the County judge. He had considered the evidence and would ride down for a preliminary hearing and make a judgement on where the trial should be held. The case appeared to be so important that it might need to be transferred to the High Court in Omaha. Meanwhile, Sheriff Olsen should keep Davidson in custody, remembering that a man is innocent until he is proved guilty.

Judge Hardy, the county judge, was arriving the day after next, and Jim Tyler declared he would be ready to meet him, and it was indeed a great honour. Even Olsen said he was ready to get up from his bed to welcome the judge, but the doctor warned him that that would be extremely unwise, and of course, Mrs Olsen agreed with him. 'That man Davidson is like a viper waiting under a cactus plant to strike at anyone within reach,' she said to her husband.

In fact, Davidson had visited Olsen, just as Jacob had predicted. He wasn't carrying fruit or anything obvious, but he came with a heap of money. It wasn't visible but everyone knew it was hovering in the air in the shape of a huge bribe.

'Good morning, my dear friend,' Davidson had said. 'I can't begin to tell you how sorry I am that this has happened to you,.'

Olsen put on a brave face and said he was sorry too, and Davidson left, and his bribe left with him.

Early next morning as Jacob and Marie were seated at breakfast Deputy Sheriff Tyler burst in looking like a fish just pulled out of a creek. 'Mr Merriweather!' he shouted, 'we have a riot on our hands! A crowd of men and women have broken into the Grand hotel and taken Davidson captive. They say they're gonna string him up right outside the hotel. What the hell are we gonna do about it?'

Jacob got up from the table and strapped on his gunbelt. 'Well, Mr Tyler, we have to stop them.'

They walked down to Main Street and looked towards the Grand hotel and sure enough there was a crowd of about thirty men and they were leading Davidson by a halter round his neck.

Jacob and the deputy strode down Main Street and they reached the crowd just as one of the tallest of the men hurled the rope over a beam projecting from the hotel.

Tyler was speechless with horror. So Jacob stepped forward and shouted, 'Stop this nonsense at once!'

The crowd froze and Jack Davidson's eyes bulged with terror.

Jacob had never thought of himself as an orator but suddenly a voice from deep inside him began to speak.

144

'Do you folk know what you're about to do?'

Nobody answered.

Jacob nodded and pointed to the man who had thrown the rope over the beam. 'You, sir, do you know you're about to commit a crime? Are you ready to face the law and your conscience after you've killed a man?'

The man opened his mouth to speak but Jacob cut in. 'No, of course not. Now stand out of my way!' He strode forward and took the halter off Davidson's neck. Davidson gasped but said nothing; he was too faint with relief.

'Now,' Jacob said in a more moderate tone. 'Deputy Tyler and I know just how you feel, but we have to abide by the law. So we're going to lock Mr Davidson up in the town jail for his own protection until the judge arrives. So I advise you all to disperse and go back to your own businesses.'

There was a moment's silence, and then a whole lot of muttering.

'That's right,' Deputy Tyler said. 'Go about your business and let the law take its course.'

'Thank you,' Jack Davidson said. 'You saved my life.'

'I didn't save your life,' Jacob said. 'I saved those folk from committing a crime.'

They locked Davidson up in the town jail to await the arrival of the judge.

CHAPTER ELEVEN

Judge Hardy was greatly esteemed throughout the County and throughout the State itself. When he arrived with two US Marshals he was greeted with some warmth by Deputy Mark Tyler, and the first thing he did was to visit Sheriff Olsen and confer with him. Then he booked into the Grand hotel where he was given one of the best rooms. In fact it was the room earlier occupied by Jack Davidson.

Judge Hardy held court in a barn behind the Grand hotel. He was a stickler for correct procedure and justice, and he looked the part: tall, and distinguished with silver grey hair that flowed down to his shoulders. He entered the court and waved the audience to be seated.

'Now,' he said to the somewhat rowdy audience, which consisted of most folk in the town, 'as you know I'm here to uphold the sword of justice.'

'The sword of justice!' someone shouted from the back of the hall. 'What the hell's that?'

Judge Hardy fixed a beady eye on the man. 'The sword of justice, sir, is what keeps us civilized so that we can live in peace and harmony. Now, bring in the accused.'

Jack Davidson had recovered his composure somewhat and he was dressed in his very best suit. He rose and bowed to the judge, and then turned to the audience and bowed again, and a chorus of howls and catcalls came from the audience. The judge beat on the desk with a hammer.

'Now, gentlemen and ladies, I will have order in this court. Anyone who causes a disturbance will be asked to leave.' Then he turned to Jack Davidson. 'Please address the court, sir. Are you Jack Davidson of the Circle Bar ranch?'

'Indeed I am, sir.'

'And you understand what you are being accused of, Mr Davidson?'

Davidson's face became tinged with purple. 'The whole thing's a tissue of lies,' he bawled.

Judge Hardy nodded, and turned to the audience. 'And who is the prosecuting lawyer in this case?'

'The whole town,' the man who had spoken earlier shouted. 'Those two innocent kids didn't deserve to die. They were just trying to make a decent living on their farm.'

The judge frowned. 'But somebody has to put forward the case for the prosecution, so please keep quiet, sir.'

There was a moment of dismayed silence. Then Jacob stood up. 'I will act as prosecuting lawyer, sir.'

There was a gasp of amazement in court.

Judge Hardy peered at Jacob through a pair of rimless spectacles. 'And who are you, sir?'

'The name's Jacob Merriweather, sir.'

'And are you a lawyer, Mr Merriweather?'

Jacob smiled. 'I'm not a qualified lawyer, sir, but I have

some training in law.'

Judge Hardy frowned and then nodded. 'Very well, Mr Merriweather, then please proceed.'

Before Jacob could speak, Davidson intervened. 'Excuse me, Mr Justice Hardy, I must object.'

'On what grounds?' the judge demanded, peering at Davidson through his rimless spectacles.

'This man is a known criminal. He rode with the killer known as Black Bart who was hanged for murder in Kansas recently.'

The judge turned to Jacob. 'Is this the truth, Mr Merriweather?'

Jacob nodded. 'It's true that I rode with Black Bart for a short time, but I parted with him as soon as I realized he enjoyed killing.' He glanced at Marie and saw she was smiling.

The judge considered for a moment. 'Objection overruled. Continue with your questions, Mr Merriweather.'

Jacob turned to Jack Davidson. 'My question is this: did you pay four of your men to kill Beth and Stan Salinger on their farm?'

Davidson turned a deeper shade of puce. 'I most certainly did not! That's an outrageous accusation!'

'So you deny paying money to those men?' Jacob asked.

Davidson breathed in hard. 'I did give them a raise. I thought they deserved it.'

'I see,' Jacob said. 'I'd like to call a witness, sir.'

'Please do so.'

'Will Mr Killop come to the front of the court.'

Killop stood up warily and stared round at the assembled people, some of whom growled, while others muttered. He looked somewhat shaken. Then he came to the front and nodded at Jacob.

'Now, Mr Killop,' Jacob said, 'please tell the court your occupation.'

Killop drew himself up to his full height and looked into the distance. 'I'm a cowhand, and I worked for Mr Davidson on the Circle Bar ranch.'

'OK,' Jacob said. 'And did Mr Davidson ever offer you extra pay?'

'Yes, he did, sir.'

'Please describe the circumstances, Mr Killop.'

Killop braced himself. 'One day last year he called Wolf and Stringer and the big guy and me into his office and offered us each two hundred dollars. Said it was a bonus.'

'Is that all he said? Jacob asked him.

Killop shivered as though a cold wind had blown through the court. 'No, sir. He said there were strings attached.'

'What kind of strings?'

Killop shrugged. 'Well, you know, strings.'

Judge Hardy intervened. 'Please tell the court what you understand by strings, Mr Killop.'

A look of weariness and defeat fell on Killop and he looked for a moment as though he might collapse. Then he pulled himself together and spoke. 'Well, what I mean is conditions, sir.'

Judge Hardy leaned forward in his chair. 'Please tell us exactly what Mr Davidson said, Mr Killop.'

Killop gulped. 'Mr Davidson said. . . .'

'Take your time, Mr Killop,' the judge cautioned. 'This is very important evidence.'

'Yes, sir,' Killop mouthed.

'The exact words, please, Mr Killop.'

Killop inhaled deeply. 'Mr Davidson's exact words were, "I want you boys to ride up to the Salinger place and put those two to silence whichever way you can".'

Davidson rose to his feet and bawled out, 'That's a complete pack of lies. This man is lying through his back teeth.'

'Why should he be doing that, Mr Davidson?' the judge asked. 'What purpose would it serve?'

'Revenge!' Davidson stormed. 'This man took my money and said he wanted more. He's a complete liar!'

'Thank you, Mr Davidson. Please sit down, sir.'

Davidson stared at Jacob and said, 'You'll pay for this. I'll see you in hell!'

Judge Hardy made a note on his notepad, and then looked up. 'Ladies and gentlemen, I think I've heard enough. Thank you for your patience. I'd like to commend Mr Merriweather on the way he has conducted the arraignment.'

He turned to Davidson who was still fuming in his chair. 'Mr Davidson, I will commit you for trial on a charge of provoking murder in the County Court in the next session. Thank you, ladies and gentlemen.' As he turned to leave there was a tumultuous cheer from the audience.

After the hearing, which was surprisingly brief, the two US marshals took charge of the prisoner and locked him in the town jail until the morning, when he would be taken to the County jail to await trial. Judge Hardy approached Jacob and Marie outside the barn. He gave Jacob a shrewd look and said, 'You did well, Mr Merriweather, and I have to admit you look more like a lawyer than a gunman. What made you change?'

Jacob bowed. 'Well, sir,' he said, 'you could say I'm a reformed character. Like I said in court, as soon as I realized Black Bart enjoyed killing I knew I'd taken the wrong track. So I decided to turn my life around.' He looked at

150

Marie. 'And then I met Miss Silversmith, who was a good friend of the murdered woman, and I had to help track down the killers and bring them to justice. So you could say Marie Silversmith reformed me.'

Judge Hardy gave a bark of laughter. 'Well, Mr Merriweather, they say it takes a good woman to make a good man, so long may it last!'

The trial in the County Court some weeks later was a different matter altogether. As soon as they entered the Court Jacob and Marie sensed a deeply hostile atmosphere. The prosecuting attorney was a good man, but Jack Davidson had hired the best defence lawyer in the business, a man well known for his skilful questioning. And, not surprisingly, Jacob saw that the principal witness for the defence was Jack Davidson's manservant Arnold, who was as smooth and slippery as a snake.

The witnesses for the prosecution were Killop, Jacob, Marie, Running Deer and Sheriff Olsen.

When Killop took the stand he seemed a lot less confident that he had in the earlier hearing. He held his head down and refused to make eye contact with anyone. He asserted that Jack Davidson had offered him and the other three two hundred dollars each for 'getting rid of the Salingers, one way or the other'.

'What did you understand by that phrase "one way or the other" Mr Killop?' the prosecuting attorney asked.

Killop stared at the floor and mumbled, 'I understood he wanted us to kill them.'

'Please speak more clearly, Mr Killop,' the prosecuting attorney demanded.

Killop looked up and his face was as pale as lard. '*He wanted us to kill them!*' he blurted out.

Then the lawyer for the defence stood up with a sardonic grin on his face. 'Are you an educated man, Mr Killop?'

'I can't say I am,' Killop replied.

'Might I suggest that you knew perfectly well what you were doing when you accepted the money?'

'I guess so.'

'And you took the money and for your own purposes.'

'Well, yes I did,' Killop mumbled.

'*Yes, you did,*' the defence attorney repeated sarcastically. 'And did it occur to you that it was rather strange that Mr Davidson had supposedly hired four men to do a job that one man could have done quite easily on his own?'

Killop opened his mouth and gulped.

'Precisely,' said the lawyer. 'I put it to you, Mr Killop, that your evidence is nothing but a pack of lies, and that when Mr Davidson gave you that money it was as a bonus, and you and those other gentlemen who are now unfortunately deceased had your own reasons for killing those Salingers?'

Killop gulped again and muttered, 'No, sir. I'm speaking the truth.'

The defence lawyer then called the manservant Arnold, who looked as well turned out as an opera goer in the opening night. 'Are you Joseph Arnold?'

A faint smile flitted across the man's lips. 'Indeed I am, sir.'

'And how long have you been employed by Mr Davidson, Mr Arnold?'

'That would be some twenty years, sir.'

'And is he a trustworthy and just employer?'

'None better, sir. I've never known him to break his word.'

'Thank you. And did you ever come across Stanley and Beth Salinger?'

The smile flickered across Arnold's face again. 'Yes, sir, I remember them both well. The young man worked on the ranch and the lady was in Mr Davidson's service in the house, and then they both disappeared one day.'

'You mean they ran away together?'

'Most probably, sir. I wouldn't know about that.'

'And what was Mr Davidson's relationship with the two?'

Arnold paused to think. 'Well, sir, Mr Davidson had no relationship with Mr Salinger. Salinger was just a wrangler who worked on the ranch on a temporary basis. As for Beth Fortune, she worked in the house for a time and then she just disappeared.'

'Is that all?' the defending attorney asked.

'I'm not quite sure what you mean, sir.'

The defending lawyer smiled enigmatically. 'Let me put it another way, Mr Arnold. Did you ever see any signs of intimacy between Mr Davidson and the young lady?'

Arnold looked deeply shocked, 'Oh, no, sir, nothing like that. She was a serving girl. Mr Davidson rarely saw her.'

The defending lawyer nodded. 'Precisely. Now, will you take your mind back to the day when Mr Davidson gave Wolf and Stringer, Killop, and the other man the two hundred dollars each. Have you any memory of that, Mr Arnold?'

Arnold smiled. 'Well, of course I remember it, I was right there standing beside Mr Davidson holding the strongbox when Mr Davidson counted out the money.'

'And did Mr Davidson say anything at the time?'

'Of course, sir.'

'And can you tell the court what he said?'

Arnold gave an almost saintly smile. 'It was like in the Holy Book. He gave them each a kind of blessing and said, "You men have done so well since you've been in my employment that I'm going to give you each a bonus. Don't squander it, but spend it wisely."' Arnold smiled benignly at the jury and a kind of awe settled on the court.

Then Killop sprang up again. 'That's a goddamn lie!' he shouted. 'He ordered us to kill those two kids!'

The judge struck the table with his gavel. 'Be silent, sir! Be silent! And sit down!'

Killop glared round the court and shouted, 'It's a damned lie, I tell you! It's a damned lie!'

Jacob and Marie and Old Sam were standing outside the courthouse.

'What's your opinion of the case so far?' Sam asked Jacob.

Jacob shook his head. 'My opinion is that that guy Arnold should be on the stage because he's the biggest actor West of Kentucky.'

'What happens if we lose the case?' Marie asked.

Jacob ran his hand over his chin. 'Well, it could be serious. We could even be charged with perjury.'

'In that case,' Sam said, 'we should lift up our voices in prayer because that's the only thing that will help with scoundrels like Arnold and Davidson, not to mention that crooked defence lawyer. But however the case goes, that man Davidson will meet his righteous Fate one way or the other.'

Old Sam's words of wisdom proved sound, and Jacob's forebodings were also confirmed. The prosecution fell apart like crumbling cheese, and when the jury retired to consider their verdict they were out for less than half an hour.

'Have you agreed on your verdict?' the judge asked when they returned.

'Yes, we have, sir,' the foreman replied.

'Do you find the accused guilty or not guilty?'

There was a dramatic pause before the foreman announced firmly, 'Not guilty, sir!'

Jacob and Marie rode back to Buffalo feeling somewhat depressed. And Sam sat high on the seat of his painted wagon. He was singing quietly to himself as though they had won a great victory. The eternal optimist!

'So, what happens when we get back to town?' he asked.

Jacob and Marie, who were riding side by side, looked at one another and smiled.

'When we get back to town,' Jacob said, 'we make ready to get married as soon as possible.'

'So,' Sam chuckled, 'every cloud does indeed have a silver lining.'

Marie was laughing. 'It's a pity you're not in holy orders, Sam. Otherwise we'd ask you to tie the knot for us.'

Sam smiled down at her through his Santa Claus beard. 'That would indeed be an honour, Miss Silversmith. Of course, I could always give you a blessing for what it's worth.'

'That would be worth a whole gold mine of marriage ceremonies,' Jacob said.

In the town there were several men of the cloth: a Jesuit named Father Louie, a Baptist minister who was well known for being somewhat straight-laced, and a preacher from England who was popular but somewhat lax in his doctrinal approach. Neither the bride nor the groom had firm ideas about religion, so they chose the preacher from England who was a tall rangy character with red whiskers and a friendly wife. Angus Modify, the preacher, lived in a somewhat ramshackle house on the outskirts of town where he held weekly services.

When Jacob and Marie knocked on the door they thought the house might fall down, but the door was opened by the friendly wife, a small, plain young woman with an honest currant-bun face.

'What can I do for you?' she asked cheerfully, but somewhat timorously.

'Is the reverend in?' Jacob asked.

'Yes, he is,' she replied. 'It's Miss Silversmith and Mr Merriweather, isn't it?'

'It is,' Jacob said. 'You're very observant, Mrs Modify.'

The Reverend Angus Modify appeared immediately. 'Please come in,' he said cheerily. 'And welcome to our humble abode, such as it is.'

It was indeed humble. They went into a long room with a desk at one end and a general living space at the other.

'Please sit down.' He waved towards two plain chairs and they sat down. He beamed benignly at Marie. 'So you want me to marry you?'

'That's why we're here,' Jacob said.

The Reverend Angus Modify was very young, certainly no older than twenty-five, and his face glowed with missionary zeal. 'Well, it will be an honour, Mr Merriweather, a great honour.'

'Indeed!' his wife crowed from the other end of the room.

*

The wedding took place after a week, without undue ceremony, or so they hoped! Jacob asked Running Deer to be his best man, and, although Running Deer had little idea of what that entailed, he agreed. Marie asked Sophie, Running Deer's wife, to be her lady in waiting, and Mrs Modify, who dressed like a Puritan, advised her on the appropriate attire. The Modifys owned a somewhat dilapidated organ from which she coaxed some kind of simple hymn tune. Old Sam produced an ancient fiddle, which he played with more gusto than musicianship. He also insisted on giving a somewhat overlong blessing full of all kinds of reference, some biblical and others somewhat more profane.

The Reverend Modify conducted the ceremony with great aplomb. He hadn't had so many people in his congregation since the beginning of his ministry, but it boded well for the future.

The people of the town turned out in their hundreds. Life was real hard in the West and everyone enjoyed a good wedding and a good funeral, in fact any opportunity to rejoice and get drunk! So the Reverend threw open the doors of his modest abode and Mrs Modify thumped away on the clapped-out organ, and Old Sam even took his fiddle out into the street where folk danced and sang bawdy songs well into the night.

But there was one notable absence – two, in fact: Sheriff Olsen and his wife. It seemed that Olsen had developed a fever, and his wife was caring for him at home where they must have heard the noise!

Next morning the whole town seemed to be asleep, quite a few of the menfolk snoring on the sidewalk or even on Main Street itself, such are the ways of mankind!

Old Sam was philosophical. He had slept in his painted wagon as usual and was walking among the living dead, bestowing blessings left and right. Then he saw Jacob and Marie emerging from Marie's cabin.

'Well, now good folks,' he said, 'So you've had your honeymoon. Where will you go for your vacation?'

'We've already decided about that,' Jacob said. 'As soon as Marie's sold her house, we're going West to Oregon where the apples grow red as the sun at sundown in high summer.'

'Well, well,' Sam smiled. 'Mr Merriweather, I do believe marriage must be good for you since it's turning you into a poet. And what will you do in Oregon when you get there?'

This time Marie spoke. 'Well now, Mr Critchley, it might be a long way ahead but I aim to run a good hotel, and Jacob here. . . .' She paused and looked at Jacob.

Jacob nodded. 'And if I can scrape enough greenbacks together I aim to start my own law business.'

'Well, sir, I hope you succeed. There's a great need for honest lawyers west of the Missouri river.' He wagged his Santa Claus beard. 'And what about a family? Do you have plans to start a family?'

'Who knows?' Jacob said with an enigmatic smile. 'Who knows?'

Old Sam had said, 'Davidson will meet his righteous fate sooner or later,' and he was right, and it came sooner than anyone had expected. Less than three months after the trial a masked rider came to the door of the Davidson ranch house. When the black servant girl answered the door, he said, 'Get out of my way, girl, unless you want to get yourself shot!'

The girl had turned and fled screaming, and Arnold had appeared, gun in hand. He fired at the masked intruder but missed. The intruder shot him in the heart and then pumped two shots into his head.

'Take that, you yellow bastard!' the intruder shouted. Then he walked through the living-room under the vulgar chandeliers and emptied his gun at the vulgar furniture. Then he drew another gun and shouted, 'Where are you, Jack Davidson, you yellow-livered bloodsucker?'

Davidson had been trying to hide behind a table, but he rose in panic and tried to climb the stairs, which was a big mistake. The gunman laughed, levelled his second gun and shot Davidson in the back. Davidson fell forward and slithered down in his own blood to the bottom of the stairs.

As the gunman stood over him, Davidson tried to turn his head. 'Mercy!' he cried.

'Mercy!' the gunman mocked. 'This is mercy, a bullet in your brain!'

And he fired twice into Davidson's head. Then he turned and laughed as he shot out the chandeliers.

A few days later an article appeared in the local news sheet. '*Rich rancher Jack Davidson shot to death in his own ranch house by an unknown gunman.*'

No one knew who the masked gunman was, and though there was much speculation, no one ever found out.

Marie managed to sell her property in town, and she and Jacob Merriweather rode West to Oregon. She did set up in the hotel business, where they sold good honest food and drink. And Jacob started his own law firm, which became well known throughout the territory. Marie and

Jacob had three children, two girls and a boy, Jacob Junior.

Old Sam stayed in the River Platte region where he plied his healing and preaching trade until the end of his days.